Room Service: Love, Lust and Lies

B. B. James

Thank you for reading my book Josie, the first of many to come. x Bev.

To whom it may concern . . .

Was that how you started a suicide note?

She really had no idea. She'd never written one before. (Obviously!) Was there some sort of protocol you were supposed to follow? Some life-ending etiquette she was unaware of?

Usually you knew who would be reading a letter, but this one was likely to be read by anyone and everyone: her friends, her family, the police, the cleaner, even.

Her lover.

No, it would have to be left open. Those involved would know who they were.

And what should it contain? An explanation? Well, that was going to be pretty clear once it all came out. She had expected them to spend the rest of their lives together. And then *she* came along.

Why was she even worrying about this? It wasn't as though she owed anything to anyone. Quite the opposite, in fact. 'Goodbye, cruel world,' wouldn't be far from the truth, but she wasn't going to be remembered for a cliché.

No, just keep it simple.

To whom it may concern.

I'm sorry if this has upset you, but there's only one person to blame for this.

Claire Frazer.

1

'Claire Frazer, you're a scheming, manipulative, selfish bitch who ought to know better.'

Claire nodded. She couldn't in all honesty disagree.

'Your Richie, he loves you to bits, doesn't he? Follows you around like a puppy. You know he'd do anything for you.'

Perhaps that's the problem, she thought.

'And yet here you are, lusting after someone almost old enough to be your father. And not only that, but he's married, for God's sake! Are you crazy? Just because he's rich and handsome and one of the country's top surg—'

The doorbell rang, interrupting Claire's argument with her reflection that she had been on the verge of losing. She checked her look in the mirror one last time – yes, it was only Jinny, but a girl had to have standards – and headed downstairs to admit her best friend.

Claire and Jinny were both well aware of their 'Odd Couple' nickname at work, but it was kindly meant and neither woman took offence. On the face of it, they had little in common, certainly not physically. Claire was a five-eight blonde glamour queen with a model's silhouette and legs to die for while Jinny, half a foot shorter, was constantly trying and failing to diet away her chubbiness.

In character, too, they were cast in very different moulds. Claire thrived on chaos, meeting life's deadlines with seconds to spare and always somehow getting away with it, no matter what the 'it' happened to be. Jinny, on the other hand, was the epitome of organization. You just knew there would always be a spare toilet roll in her loo. An odd couple for sure, but Jinny was the steadying hand on the tiller of Claire's speedboat existence, and, although she would never tell her as much, Claire knew that without her friend's guidance her life might very easily slip out of control.

Claire was always happy to see Jinny, but especially so tonight, for there was a particularly burning issue she wanted to discuss. Jinny had protested at Claire's suggestion of a girls' night in on a Monday, when they both had to be up for work in the morning, but had soon agreed once Claire gave her the pouty-mouthed 'Please, please, *pleeease*' that always seemed to get results with everyone she employed it on.

Everyone except the one person she really wanted to bewitch, that was.

'Jinny, sweetheart! It's so lovely to see you!' Claire kissed the air somewhere in the region of Jinny's left cheek.

'Um, we only left the unit two hours ago,' said Jinny, laughing.

'I know, I know, but that's just work. Starch and disinfectant. It's been ages since we had a proper catch-up. Come on through. I've got claret!'

Jinny hung her duffel coat on a hook in the hallway and followed her friend upstairs and into the lounge, where Claire had already poured two glasses of wine. They toasted each other and sat at either end of the squashy black leather settee that dominated the small room. Jinny delved into the canvas shopping bag that she always carried with her and placed a home-made quiche, a six-pack of Wotsits and two Tupperware containers of sandwiches on Claire's coffee table.

'I thought I'd bring something to soak up the wine,' she

explained. 'I don't suppose you've got anything for us to eat on our "girls' night in"?'

'Er, no actually,' said Claire, 'unless Weetabix counts. But I have got two more bottles in the kitchen!'

She opened one of the plastic containers and started chewing enthusiastically. 'Mmmm, these are great. I didn't have time for lunch and I'm starving!' She held out the open box. 'Want one?'

Jinny shook her head – 'Maybe later' – and looked enviously at her friend's flat stomach, shown off by the knotted check blouse she wore over a pair of skimpy white shorts that displayed her permatanned legs to perfection. Her pink-painted fingernails shone bright against the brown of her thighs.

'You're so lucky,' she said. 'I only have to look at a cream cake and I go up a dress size, but you seem to be able to eat what you like. You even manage to look great in your uniform. "The Woman in Blue", they call you. You know, like that film that's just come out.'

Claire looked at her blankly.

'The one with Kelly LeBrock and Gene – oh, never mind.

Let's just say you've got a lot more in common with her than with me.'

'I wish you'd stop putting yourself down, Jinny. You're kind and funny and clever and reliable. And married to someone who worships the ground you walk on. *You're* the lucky one. In fact, I really need your help with something. I'm in a terrible predicament and I just don't know what to do. If I don't sort it out I'm going to die!'

A look of horror crossed Jinny's face. 'Die? Oh God, Claire, don't say that! What is it? Are you ill? Surely there must be something they can –'

'No, I don't mean *die* die, silly. That's just a figment of speech. I –'

'Well if you don't mean it then don't say it,' snapped Jinny. 'You almost gave me a heart attack then. Can't you ever think before you speak? And it's "figure".'

Claire had no idea what Jinny was referring to but decided that silence would be golden for the time being. This wasn't going as planned at all. *For a clever person, Claire Frazer, you can be very stupid at times*, she thought to herself.

And, no doubt about it, she *was* clever. Growing up, she had harboured dreams of stage and screen stardom but her mother had wisely told her to use the brain she'd been blessed with and forge a proper career for herself. She had chosen healthcare, and emerged from university with a surprisingly good nursing degree and an equally surprising amount of enthusiasm for the profession. Now, at the age of twenty-six, she was the youngest head of department at Harvington General, managing the hospital's post-operative recovery unit with great acuity and foresight. Staff and patients both liked and admired her because, despite her at times infuriatingly haphazard approach to life, she was damn good at her job, even if she did say so herself.

Although her love of medicine had arisen not only because nurses were supposed to be sexy and doctors rich and handsome, it was that aspect of her vocation that was causing her untold grief now, and the reason she was in such desperate need of Jinny's wisdom.

'I'm sorry if I upset you, Jinny. I really didn't mean to.'

'I know,' Jinny sighed. 'I just wish –'

'Hey, did you notice the state of Maria this morning? Hair all over the place and yawning her head off. She had a date with a new fella yesterday. I don't reckon she did much sleeping last night!'

'Oh, Claire, you're terrible,' said Jinny with a laugh as Claire topped up both their glasses. 'Not everyone's like you, you know. Actually, that quiche does look nice. Have you got a knife?'

The two women spent the next hour gossiping their way through Jinny's provisions and another bottle of wine until Claire finally felt able to return to the main reason she had asked Jinny round.

That reason was Hugo Bowman, a tall, fair-haired, cricket-playing orthopaedic consultant for whom Claire had had the hots ever since he'd joined Harvey General's surgical team the previous month. He oozed sex appeal and charm, and all the girls at work fancied him like mad, though Claire suspected most of them would run a mile if he ever actually showed an interest in them.

'Jinny,' she said casually as she opened another bottle, 'you know that problem I was telling you about earlier?'

Jinny nodded.

'Well, I was wondering, have you ever had an affair?'

'Oh, yes, dozens,' replied Jinny, who was now rather tipsy.

Claire almost choked on her wine. That was the last thing she'd expected to hear.

'Bryan Ferry, Paul Newman, that bloke from A-Ha,' she continued. 'I've had the lot. All in my head, of course. I'd never do anything against my Brian. Ahh, my lovely Brian, he's a sweetheart, isn't he?'

Claire realised she her friend had probably consumed rather too much claret to conduct a sensible conversation, but, reasoning that the principle of *in vino veritas* might actually work to her advantage, decided to press on with her plan.

'Jinny Robinson, I'm shocked! You're a bit of a dark horse, aren't you?' she said, her admiration not entirely feigned.

'You're not the only one with a dildo hidden in your bedside drawer, you know.' Jinny giggled, pleased at her friend's reaction, then put her hand to her mouth. 'Oh my God, did I really just say that? Claire, you mustn't tell Brian;

promise me you won't.'

'Of course not. This is girls' talk, Jinny. Nothing we say goes beyond these four walls. But there is something I'd like to know, if you don't mind me asking. It would really help me with my problem.'

'You're my best buddy, Claire,' said Jinny, moving along the settee to take her friend's hand. 'You know you can ask me anything.'

'I know you were only joking just now about having affairs, but, seriously, in real life, what would it take to actually make you be unfaithful to Brian?'

'Nothing. There's nothing, Claire,' said Jinny, serious and sober now. 'He's my world. We're trying for a baby, did I tell you?'

She hadn't, but Claire had more pressing matters on her mind than to pursue the subject.

'Really, Jinny? Think about it; there must be someone who could prise you away from him. Someone you really like.'

'Absolutely not, Claire. No one could split me and my Brian up.'

Claire frowned. That wasn't what she'd wanted to hear.

'Unless . . .'

'What, Jinny? Unless what?'

'Well, I suppose unless I found out Brian wasn't the person I thought he was.'

'What, like he was the Yorkshire Ripper or something?'

'Goodness, Claire, everything's always so dramatic with you,' replied Jinny with a laugh. 'No, I mean if I found out he'd been having an affair himself or was already married to someone else, something like that.'

'Oh, right,' said Claire slowly, 'I see what you mean.'

'But that's never going to happen,' said Jinny confidently. 'Brian and me, we're for life. No one could replace Brian, except . . .'

'Go on,' said Claire, sensing a breakthrough.

'Except another Brian!' Jinny giggled.

'I should have guessed,' said Claire. 'You're the perfect couple. So lucky . . .'

'What is it, Claire?' asked Jinny. 'Something's wrong, isn't it? Is it Richie? What's he done?'

Claire almost laughed at the thought that Richie would ever two-time her. As she had told herself earlier, he loved her to bits. In the six months they had been going out together he had treated her with nothing but love and kindness. Two years her senior, he was good looking, considerate, attentive, had a steady job with prospects – everything a girl could ask for, to be honest. But somehow it just wasn't enough.

'It's not Richie, Jinny. It's Hugo.'

'Hugo?' Jinny looked nonplussed for a moment before realisation dawned. You mean Hugo *Bowman*? From the hospital? *That* Hugo?'

'Yes, Jinny, that Hugo.'

'Good grief! Don't tell me that you and he are –'

'No, we're not. That's the trouble. I'm not sure he even knows my name.' She picked up her wine glass, then, realising both it and the last bottle were empty, replaced it. 'Look, Jinny, I know this sounds mad, but I think I'm in love with him.'

Spoken aloud, the notion sounded ridiculous even to her, but whenever they crossed paths at work she became overwhelmed by his physical presence and almost hypnotised by the aroma of his aftershave. She had even bought Richie a bottle of the same brand for his birthday.

'He's just – I don't know – he has such a *presence*, Jinny.'

The appointment of Hugo Bowman that July had been a real coup for Harvington General. After five years in medical school following his graduation from Oxford, he had honed his surgical expertise at a top London hospital and was now considered one of the country's leading orthopaedic surgeons. Unlike many of his contemporaries, rather than heading exclusively to private practice, where the big bucks were guaranteed, he had opted to include the dimmer lights of the NHS among his clientele and had a regular list slot at Harvington.

Jinny swirled the wine in her glass thoughtfully. 'Even I can see he's attractive, but *love*?' she said. 'Are you being serious, Claire, or is this just the drink talking? We've both had rather a lot, after all.'

'I wish it was,' said Claire. 'I've tried so hard to fight it' – not strictly true, she reflected; in fact she hadn't tried very hard at all – 'but I just can't. He and I were made for each other,

Jinny, I know it.'

'Oof! Where has all this come from?' said Jinny. 'I thought you and Richie were solid.'

'We were. We are. Richie's a great guy, and I know he'd do anything for me. And I do love him. Or I did. But since Hugo came to work here I haven't been able to think about anything else. It's driving me crazy!'

'Well, I can see how your head might be turned,' said Jinny. 'He does look more like a film star that a doctor. He told me I was the best department clerk he'd ever worked with,' she added proudly. 'And I know he respects you as a lead nurse. I overheard him saying to the director of nursing how professional you are on the ward.'

'Really?' That was a start, at least.

'Yes. But, Claire – he's a married man!'

'I know, I know!' Claire slouched back on the sofa and sighed as she scraped her blonde hair back from her face and held it for a minute. 'But I just feel like I could do with a bit of – I don't know – fun. I'm on a treadmill at the moment. I've had enough.'

'Enough of the job, or enough of Richie?' asked Jinny.

'I don't know. Maybe both,' answered Claire.

'Claire, you can get a job anywhere. I wouldn't want you to leave, but you don't have to stay at Harvington, and you don't have to stay with Richie either, even though I think you'd be a fool not to.'

Claire threw her head back. 'I know. He's lovely, but he's so possessive, and keeps going on about what a wonderful future we're going to have. I mean, what is there to look forward to – a house to clean, kids to run round after? There must be more to life than that. It might be good enough for –' She tried to breathe the words back in but it was too late.

'Good enough for me and Brian, is that what you were going to say?' asked Jinny.

'Jinny, I'm so sorry. I didn't –'

But for some reason Jinny was smiling rather than furious. 'Don't you see, Claire, that's exactly the point; it's perfectly good enough for Brian and me. It's what we both want and it makes us happy. I'm not angry; I'm just sad that you can't want the same. Obviously Richie does.'

'You're right, of course. He's never actually asked me to marry him, thank God, but he's always hinting that we should settle down together and start a family. I just keep changing the subject.'

'That's you, Claire. Me, I'm quite content with that. I'm not pregnant yet, but hopefully I soon will be. I love my job, and we have the mortgage together, we have our holiday breaks, what more would I want? I think you'd be a fool to give all that up, and especially for an affair with a married man. You say you love Mr Bowman, but you don't even know him, not really. Trust me, if you throw yourself at him, it's going to end in tears.' Jinny finished the last of her wine and looked at her watch. 'Good Lord, it's one o'clock! I'd better call a cab. Brian will be wondering where I've got to.'

'At least he'll know you're not cheating on him,' said Clare ruefully as she picked up the phone. 'Richie probably has a spy outside the . . . Oh, yes, hello. Could we have a taxi from 13a Well Street, please? It's the flat above Deakin's Antiques.'

The cab arrived almost immediately and Jinny grabbed her bag and headed downstairs to the hallway, flicking her short dark brown hair into place with her hand as she walked to the door. She gave her friend a hug and a worried look. 'Claire, I shouldn't be telling you this but . . .'

'What? You can't stop now.'

'I think Mr Bowman might already be, you know, seeing someone. I've seen them holding hands and having a quick kiss when they thought no one was looking.'

'Who, Jinny? Who's he seeing?'

'Rebecca Maine,' said Jinny. 'Of course, I might have got it all wrong, so don't tell anyone, will you?'

The taxi driver revved his engine impatiently.

'Just think about what you've got, Claire, before you throw it away,' Jinny called over her shoulder as she hurried to the waiting car.

Claire closed the door and stood with her back against it, reflecting on the night's events. Should she pity Jinny or envy her? And Hugo was already cheating on his wife! Was that a good or a bad thing? She couldn't decide. The evening hadn't been a complete failure – she certainly knew more now than she had at the start of it – but was Jinny right? Was the grass really no greener on the other side of the fence?

She caught sight of her reflection in the hallway mirror.

'I guess there's only one way to find out, isn't there?' she asked herself.

She locked up, switching off and unplugging, splashing her face with warm water before falling into bed, her decision made. Within minutes, she was sound asleep.

2

Claire woke to the buzzing of her alarm clock, something that always irritated her. She punched the off button and lay for a few more minutes, resurfacing, and then a few more. Hearing the church clock strike seven, she leapt from her bed and rushed to the shower in a panic.

Five minutes later and still towelling herself down with one hand, she quickly blasted her hair with the dryer, muttering to herself about the inhumanity of early-morning starts and the fact that Tuesday was the busiest day of the week in her department. Luckily, her hair was in good shape. She piled it up, artfully leaving a few strands to fall naturally. She quickly applied her foundation, donned her sunglasses to hide her unshadowed eyes and grabbed her make-up bag so that she could finish the job later. An illegally rapid dash to work in her blue-and-white Mini Cooper saw her arriving with seconds to spare before her shift began at 7.45 a.m. Satisfied that the staff of the recovering anaesthetics room she led were all present and correct, she decided to use her 'Just have to chase up a drug delivery' excuse to slip away to the locker room and complete her make-up routine. Before she could make her escape, though, she was intercepted by Libby Hancock, her senior staff nurse.

'Morning, Claire,' Libby said in greeting. 'Here's today's list. Good night last night? Jinny said you had a girls' night in.'

'Er, yes, not bad,' replied Claire distractedly, checking the list Libby had just given her. 'Have all these morning cases been seen and premedicated?' she asked, running her finger down the first six names on the sheet of paper, all of whom were due to undergo routine procedures. Tuesday was the day scheduled for elective orthopaedic surgery, and Hugo Bowman's efficiency and reputation meant that the day's list was always chock-a-block.

'Yes indeed,' replied Libby. 'Checked and ready to go. Baseline observations all satisfactory. Lyn has just gone to fetch the first one up from the ward.'

'Great! I'll be back in five minutes,' said Claire. 'I just have to chase up . . .' The end of her sentence was lost as she charged off to the locker room. On the way, she passed Jinny's office, where her friend gave her a disapproving look from behind her desk and pointed to her watch. Even after a late night out, Jinny was always in on time the next morning. She was the early bird preparing for the day ahead with a large mug of coffee to hand.

It crossed Claire's mind to offer her own reprimand for gossiping with Libby about their evening, but that would have to wait. She was sure, anyway, that Jinny would never divulge anything said to her in confidence. She might have been a chatterbox, but she was utterly trustworthy with a secret. Claire emerged within minutes looking just as the staff were used to seeing her – fully made up and glamorous, and trailing in her wake a hint of the latest film-star-endorsed perfume. This morning there was a spring in her step, because, for obvious reasons, the orthopaedic list was her favourite.

On the way back to her department she passed Lyn Hawes walking alongside the first patient of the day, an elderly gentleman who was looking rather nervous as he was being wheeled to theatre. 'Good morning, Sister Frazer,' Lyn said, careful to avoid over familiarity in front of the clientele, something Claire had had to remind her to do on more than one occasion.

Claire responded with an approving smile. 'Good morning, Nurse Hawes.' Her mind flashed back to the list Libby had shown her earlier. Claire's life might have been the epitome of chaos outside work, but once in uniform she became scalpel sharp. 'And this must be Mr Lewis. We're giving you a new hip today, Mr Lewis, aren't we?'

'That's right, Sister,' he said. 'I'm a bit worried they're going to do the wrong one.'

Claire took the old man's hand in hers. 'I can assure you that's never going to happen, Mr Lewis. You're being operated on by Mr Bowman, who is probably the best orthopaedic surgeon in the land. He doesn't make mistakes.' Apart from not falling head over heels for her, of course. 'It will all be over in no time, and before you know it you'll be waking up to find Nurse Hawes here looking after you.'

The man smiled up at her gratefully. 'Thank you.'

'Off you go, then. Can't keep our star surgeon waiting.'

Back on the ward, Claire made a tray of coffees. Although she was a stickler for medical detail and protocol, she wasn't the sort to treat those she managed as lackeys, and was more than happy to take her turn at the kettle. She usually made a cup for Jinny, even though she wasn't part of Claire's team. Claire had a lot of professional respect for her friend, who was good at her job as well as good natured. Besides, department clerks always seemed to know what was going on everywhere in the hospital, which made them very useful allies.

An hour later, Mr Lewis arrived in the recovery room and the day's real work began. Lyn stayed with him until he was fully alert and ready to return to the ward. Claire took care of the next patient herself, an Indian lady who had undergone a shoulder arthroscopy. She thought it was important not to expect her staff to do anything she couldn't or wouldn't do herself, and this hands-on attitude had earned her a great deal of respect and admiration. Her very presence, and how she managed herself and the patients, generated enthusiasm and motivation and inspired the whole recovery room. Whenever there were difficulties, the staff would pull together collectively.

Under Claire's leadership they were a strong team, with a sense of responsibility, pride and motivation to succeed. She just wished that she could bring some of that efficiency into her own life, and especially her love life.

A porter arrived to return Mr Lewis to the ward, and Lyn went with them to report on his condition to the ward staff. Claire waved him on his way from her own patient's bedside as the next one appeared through the doors connecting the room to the theatre corridor. Harvington General had been built only twenty years ago, and the twelve-bed recovery room was well appointed, with oxygen terminals spaced along the walls. The air-exchange system worked efficiently, and the room was equipped with everything that the nursing staff and medics needed to enable patients to recover quickly and fully from anaesthetisation. It was the responsibility of Claire's senior nurse to ensure that the room was cleaned thoroughly, and so far Libby had never let her boss down.

'Amanda?' Claire called across to her latest student nurse, who had started her rotation there the previous day. 'Could you phone Kingfisher Ward for Mrs Chatterjee's return, please?

Then come with me for the handover.'

The young girl smiled her assent, pleased to have been given something useful to do.

The handover completed, Claire sent the student nurse on ahead while she popped into Jinny's office near the transfer bay.

'Hello,' said Jinny. 'I guess this means it's time for a coffee.'

'Sounds good to me,' said Claire. The office was placed midway between the operating theatres and the recovery room, enabling the entrances to both areas to be seen, but as they sipped their Douwe Egberts and speculated further on Maria da Sousa's love life there was only one thing Claire was monitoring: the doors to the theatre in which Hugo Bowman was currently operating.

He appeared midway through their third cup, and turned towards the recovery room.

'Anyway, as I was saying to Brian –'

'Hold that thought, Jinny,' said Claire. 'I'll be right back.'

She slipped into the corridor to intercept him.

'Hello, Mr Bowman. Might I have a word?'

The surgeon stopped and smiled.

'Sister Frazer. How can I help?'

By telling me you've booked us into a hotel for the night, thought Claire, before realising that the image now filling her head had just driven what she had planned to say completely out of it.

'Um, I just wanted to congratulate you on Mr Lewis's new hip,' she improvised lamely. 'Very, er, it was a very neat piece of work.'

'Neat, eh?' He replied with a bemused expression. 'Well, I'll be sure to tell my registrar. It was he who sewed him up.'

Claire wished for the ground to open up and swallow her, but the floor beneath her remained stubbornly unyielding as the object of her affection strode away.

3

Friday mornings at Harvington General were when the heads of department met to discuss the hospital's latest admissions and ongoing cases. The hospital's speciality was orthopaedics, so it fell to Hugo to head the multidisciplinary team meetings. From the corridor, Claire watched him approach the medical room, studying sheaf of patients' notes in his hand.

Ten minutes earlier Rebecca Maine, his theatre staff nurse and, according to Jinny, his mistress, had been in the staff kitchen preparing a tray of china cups and premium biscuits for the MDT to munch on while they deliberated. Claire had decided it was time she found out a bit more about her rival, who had only been appointed a few weeks previously but had already, it seemed, beaten her to the punch.

'Oh, hi,' said Claire as she entered. 'I'm dying for a cuppa. Sorry, I didn't realise anyone was in here.' She crossed the room and switched on the kettle. 'It's Rebecca, isn't it? I'm Claire, Claire Frazer, from –'

'From the recovery room. Yes, I know. Mr Bowman has mentioned you.'

'Really? All good, I hope,' said Claire, praying he hadn't told her what a fool she'd made of herself three days earlier.

'He says you're very efficient. That's a quality he sets great store by. He's a lovely man, but he can be a tyrant in theatre. I have to anticipate his every move during an operation, almost as if I'm carrying out the surgery myself. He expects me to have the instruments at the ready before he even asks for them.'

'And he expects you to make his coffee too?' Claire said.

'Ha ha, no, not really. But he does like to have everything just so for the MDT meeting and I sort of volunteered to make sure everything's in its right place before it starts. I'm just getting the bigwigs' nibbles ready now.'

'I'll leave you to it, then. It's been lovely to meet you,' said Claire, heading for the door.

'What about your cuppa . . . ?' said Rebecca, but she was talking to thin air.

Now, as Claire saw Hugo walking towards the meeting room, she moved quickly, arriving at the doorway a fraction before him. The fresh scent of filtered coffee wafted out as the percolator bubbled and hissed at the back of the room.

'Good morning, Mr Bowman.'

'Sister Frazer,' he replied, looking up. 'What brings you here?'

'Well, I know I'm not part of the multidisciplinary team, but I was wondering whether you'd mind if I sat in on the meeting. I think it's important to know as much about every patient in my care as possible, and if I'm aware exactly how their treatment plans have been formulated, it will enable me to work that much more efficiently.' From the corner of her eye Claire could see Rebecca approaching with the laden tray.

'That's very commendable, Sister,' Hugo said, clearly impressed. 'Please, feel free to join us.'

'Thank you so much, Mr Bowman. After you.' Claire stood with her back to the open door, leaving just enough room for the surgeon to sidle through. Was it her imagination, or did his eyes linger on hers for a second longer than necessary as he passed her?

'You're welcome,' he said, turning back to look at her.

'And, please, call me Hugo.'

***

'So, what do you think?' asked Jinny, three hours later. 'What about IVF? We should try it, yes?'

This wasn't the first time a lunch-hour chat had revolved around Jinny's failure to conceive. 'I'm really not sure,' said Claire, studying Jinny's face. 'It's such a new treatment, and really expensive, even if you can get it. I should wait a while. You've only been trying ten months.'

'Mm,' replied Jinny doubtfully. 'Mind you, I am getting on a bit, Claire.'

'Getting on? Oh, come off it, Jinny,' she said, laughing. 'OK, so the midwives may say you're older than usual to be a primigravida, but you're not past it yet, not at twenty-seven!'

Jinny, feeling ridiculed now, rose to the bait. 'Primi wotta? What's that when it's at home? Have I got something wrong with me?' Her face was flushed, but she looked intrigued all the same.

'No, stupid. It's when a woman is pregnant for the first time. Anyway, enough about that. This morning I –'

'Oh, I see,' interrupted Jinny, still intrigued. 'Older than usual. Does that mean I'm still OK to get pregnant? I don't want to have . . . you, know, complications.'

'For God's sake, Jinny, just get your legs in the air, do the deed as often as Brian can manage it and you'll be fine,' Claire said, exasperated at being unable to send the conversation in the direction she wanted.

Claire's sudden volume sent Jinny into mock panic mode. 'Shh, not so loud!' she whispered. 'You're the only one that knows we're trying for a baby, remember?' She playfully kicked out at Claire, deliberately missing her friend's calves. 'Anyway, how would you know? You're still a spinster!'

'Bloody cheek!' said Claire. 'For one thing, I don't want kids – not yet, anyway. I hear enough horror stories from that lot in there!' she added, pointing to the recovery-room staff. 'And I'm not likely to attract you know who's attention if I'm wearing a maternity dress, am I?'

'Attract whose attention?' asked Libby, who had just entered the office. 'Never mind,' she continued, before Claire could answer. 'I probably don't want to know. Come on,

Claire, it's inspection time.'

As they returned to the recovery room, Claire reflected on Libby's calm authority. She had to admit that her deputy would probably have made a better lead nurse than she was herself, but Libby was perfectly happy to forgo both the status and the responsibility of heading the unit. In some ways, Claire envied her certitude, though not her lack of ambition.

Claire and Libby visited each of the recovery bays in turn, topping up the diminishing number of airway mouthpieces along with other vital equipment necessary for patient safety in the crucial minutes following an operation. Claire enjoyed their rounds together, during which she would pick Libby's brains about current affairs, the latest fashions, the property ladder, social trends and haute cuisine. Libby came from an upper-class family whereas Claire had risen from a working-class background into a middle-class job. She sometimes felt intimidated by Libby's cultured lifestyle and privileged education, but Claire was nothing if not ambitious, and did not hesitate to use Libby's knowledge as a vehicle on her upwardly mobile journey. What she really needed to complete the transition, though, was a husband with a profession. Richie had his good points, but his job as a sales manager, though decent enough, wasn't going to cut it. Someone like Hugo would certainly fit the bill as husband material. Unfortunately, he was already someone else's. Still, Rebecca Maine proved that that particular fortress might still be stormed. She would just have to think like a general on the battlefield; treat his seduction as though it were a military procedure.

All she had to do was formulate the right strategy.

4

Friday nights were always busy at the Liquor Clinic, as Harvey General's staff social club was popularly known, and particularly so tonight, as most of the off-duty staff had decided to attend Len McClure's fiftieth birthday celebration there. Len had spent the previous month handing out invites to all and sundry with an assurance that the first drink was on him, a generous impulse Claire wondered if he might now be regretting as Richie escorted her to the club's entrance door and swung it open to reveal a packed interior. A blast of 'Agadoo' escaped through the doorway, wafted on a cloud of cigarette smoke.

Len was both well liked and much discussed. There was no doubt about it, Harvington General's senior operating department assistant was damn good at his job, which was to support patients from beginning to end of their surgical procedures and ensure that all the operating-theatre equipment was well maintained. He was also an alcoholic, as evidenced by his bright red nose and pitted face. He somehow still managed to excel at his job and remain focused, but Claire – no mean drinker herself – wondered how long he could maintain the balancing act.

Claire spotted Jinny waving at her from the far side of the room, where she was sitting with Brian. The two couples often met up after work, but tonight Libby and her husband, Malcolm, a Royal Navy lieutenant home on leave from his latest tour of duty, were joining them. Richie and Claire were, as usual, the last to arrive.

'Get the drinks in, Rich. Len's paying,' she said, and headed in her friends' direction, leaving Richie to fight his way to the bar.

Heads turned, as they always did, as Claire made her way through the crowd. She wore a brown leather miniskirt, a zippered waistcoat top to match and high-heeled brown court shoes. She looked stunning, her blonde hair and deep tan completing her carefully crafted Bond-girl look. She was disappointed to see that Jinny had chosen tight black leather trousers and a ruffled cream lace blouse, a combination that emphasised both her too-ample curves and her diminutive stature.

'Hi, Claire,' said Brian. 'You look nice. Doesn't Jinny look a picture in her new outfit?'

He put his arm round Jinny's shoulder and gave her a peck on the cheek.

More like a horror movie, thought Claire, almost but not quite ashamed that the bitchy response had been the first thing to enter her mind. At least she hadn't said it out loud.

'Malcolm!' she said, turning to Libby's husband. 'We haven't seen you for ages. Have you been somewhere nice?'

'Can't say, I'm afraid, Claire. Warmer than the South Atlantic, anyway.'

'It must have been awful in the Falklands,' said Jinny. 'You *are* brave.'

'Just doing what we're paid for, Jinny. Luckier than some, eh Libs?'

Libby smiled and took his hand. 'I'm always relieved when he arrives home safely,' she said. 'You just never know what's round the corner these days, do you?'

'Where's Richie with those drinks?' said Claire, who was finding all this domestic bliss hard to swallow.

'Here,' said Richie into her ear, making her jump.

He put their drinks on the table and shook hands with the lieutenant and Brian. Inevitably the men were soon discussing the following day's First Division fixture list while the women were talking shop. By nine o'clock, the rest of Claire's staff from the late shift had arrived. Everyone seemed to have to shout louder to be heard as the volume of the music increased to match the volume of people in the club. At nine fifteen Libby and Malcolm got up to leave.

'It's a bit raucous for us,' said Libby. 'I think we'll make our way home. I'll see you on Monday, Claire.'

'Lucky you. I'm on shift tomorrow,' said Claire, standing to give her a hug.

'Perhaps you should call it a night too, then,' said Libby as the pair moved away.

But Claire had other ideas, for over Libby's shoulder she had caught sight of Hugo Bowman standing at the bar, chatting to Len McClure. She waved in their direction, her

'Hi, Len,' being swallowed up by the loud music before it could reach them.

As she'd hoped, Hugo noticed the movement and turned to look across at her while Len drank on regardless. Claire, her back to her companions, returned his stare provocatively, flicking her hair and retrieving a gold chain from her cleavage, enjoying the tease.

Suddenly Hugo left his position at the bar and started walking directly towards her. Claire was panicking slightly now. What was he going to do? What had she expected him to do? Too late, she realised hadn't thought this through at all. She was with Richie tonight. Things could get ugly. She stood like a rabbit in headlights as Hugo came ever nearer.

'You look drop-dead gorgeous.'

How had Hugo said that without moving his mouth? It took her a moment to understand that the words came not from Hugo but from Jinny, who had been watching Claire's display to the room from behind, unaware of its true purpose.

'Has everyone who wanted to taken your picture now? If so, then come and sit down,' she added with a giggle.

41

'Jinny, I think you might have had one Cinzano too many,' said Brian.

Claire looked round in embarrassment. Even Richie was grinning. Well, he wouldn't be in a minute when Hugo arrived.

But when she turned again to meet her fate, all she saw was Hugo's back, heading towards the men's toilets further down their side of the room.

'It's all right, Brian,' said Richie. 'Jinny didn't mean anything by it. I know Claire can be a bit of a show-off, can't you, darling?'

'I can fight my own battles, Rich, thanks very much,' Claire snapped, annoyed at his unsolicited defence. 'Could you get me another drink, please?'

Hugo had returned from the gents and was now sitting with Tim Dawson, his registrar, and some of the theatre staff – Rebecca Maine among them. As Richie arrived with their drinks, Hugo looked across at Claire again. Her earlier scare forgotten, Claire discreetly lowered the zip of her top a little and tugged as if to straighten it. She shook her hair to one side and reached down for her bag to get a cigarette, exposing her cleavage but careful this time to avoid eye contact with Hugo.

The room seemed to explode with noise. 'Last orders, please, ladies and gentlemen!' shouted Steve the barman, waving an old school bell. Even over the music, the clangour was deafening.

Brian and Richie took off once again for the bar, leaving Claire and Jinny alone.

'Claire, I'm sorry if I upset you earlier,' said Jinny.

'Oh, it wasn't you, Jinny, not really,' she said, and then explained what had happened. 'I really thought Hugo was going to come over here and drag me away by my hair like a cave man or something.'

The image of Claire being towed across the room by Hugo sent them both into fits of giggles, which didn't subside as the men returned. Richie and Brian were puzzled by their private joke.

'Look at the state of you, Claire. How many have you had?' asked Richie.

Claire leaned over in the chair and looked up at him from an angle. 'Ugh, cheek, you bought them,' she retorted.

'I should watch him, Claire,' said Jinny, mock seriously. 'He just wants his wicked way with you. Do you want your wicked way with me, Brian?' Jinny ruffled his dark hair, and her brown eyes shone with happiness.

'All right, calm down,' said Brian, his face red with embarrassment.

'What? I'm right, aren't I, Claire? They want to get us drunk and make babies,' she added playfully.

'I'm not *that* drunk,' said Claire with a hiccup.

'And what's that supposed to mean?' asked Richie.

'Nothing. It doesn't mean anything. Mwah!' she replied.

Richie raised his eyes to the ceiling. 'See what I have to put up with?'

'Why don't we get a takeaway and go back to mine?' suggested Jinny.

'Good idea,' said Brian, raising his glass.

'Why not?' agreed Richie.

'Yup, 's a good idea,' Claire nodded in agreement as she put down her glass and stood, swaying slightly. 'Just going to the loo. I'll catch you up.'

As the other three left, Claire, who was nowhere near as tipsy as she was pretending to be, made sure she passed Hugo's table on the way out, brushing past him as closely as she could without making it obvious. 'Oh, sorry, Mr Bowman. There's no room at all in here, is there?'

'I suppose that depends on what you're trying to do, Sister Frazer,' he said with a smile. 'I trust you've had an enjoyable evening?'

As she walked away she could sense the stares of both Hugo and Rebecca boring into her back, though for very different reasons. She had always been aware of the power of her good looks, and now so were they. The juke box had fallen silent, and on her way out a wolf whistle split the air, but it spiked no panic this time, for she knew the whistler would be Len – reacting, as was his habit, to what he thought people were thinking. He was usually right.

She called across a 'happy birthday' to him, thanked him for the drink and walked out into the darkness.

* * *

The cool September air soon sobered up the foursome as they

ordered their Chinese by numbers and asked the takeaway owner to phone for a taxi, a Friday-night task he was well used to fulfilling. Twenty minutes later they were back at Jinny and Brian's – a Victorian two-bedroomed terrace house that was eagerly waiting for a baby to arrive.

As the men took the food into the kitchen, Jinny motioned for Claire to follow her upstairs. 'Come on, I want to show you something,' she whispered, opening a door off the tiny landing. 'This will be our nursery.' The second bedroom had been painted pale yellow for either sex; the carpet was a rich cream. There were cute teddy-bear pictures with pinewood frames, one in each alcove and one on the chimney breast above the fireplace. A piggy bank stood on the mantlepiece and softly draped pale blue curtains depicting nursery-rhyme images epitomised their ambitious family planning. A cot stood in the centre of the room.

'Come on, let's get sorted,' Brian was saying as they returned downstairs, emerging from the kitchen with plates and cutlery.

The house had a cottagey feel to it – very cosy and quaint,

with old-fashioned fireplaces and sash windows. The modern gadgets inside were a stark contrast to the house's overall ambience, but somehow the mixing of old and new worked well. The music system was modern, and soft lighting in the dining room made it an ideal space for entertaining.

Jinny placed a jug of water and four glasses on the table. 'Or does anyone fancy a nightcap at all?' she asked. Brian looked across at her with a 'really?' expression; Claire and Richie remained diplomatically silent. 'Perhaps not, then,' she decided, embarrassed. 'Let's have some music.'

With the flick of a switch, the room was filled with soft and romantic love songs.

'Brian made this tape for me,' said Jinny proudly.

'I don't suppose you've got any Bruce Springsteen,' said Richie, followed by 'Ow!' as Claire kicked him under the table.

After the meal, the girls made coffees and the four friends relaxed, chatting and joking until two in the morning.

'God, I have to be at work in six hours!' said Claire. 'It's my Saturday on. Richie, we'd better go.'

'You're welcome to stay over, you know,' said Brian. 'It's

only a camp bed but –'

'No, it's OK, thanks, but we had better get back to Claire's,' said Richie.

The taxi arrived and they said their goodbyes. From the back seat Claire could see Brian and Jinny embracing behind the glazed front door before heading towards the stairs, no doubt for another attempt at baby-making. Perhaps this would be her friend's lucky night.

'Just along here, by the antiques shop,' said Richie as the taxi turned into Well Lane. 'I'll stay tonight, shall I?' asked Richie, as he paid the driver. 'Round things off nicely?'

Claire was hardly enthusiastic, but since she hadn't opened her purse all evening she didn't feel able to refuse. He was horny and she was uninterested, but at two in the morning, she was in no fit state to begin making other arrangements. She knew that Richie wouldn't press her, appreciating that she had to be up early. And anyway, cuddling up to a warm body didn't seem like such a bad idea.

5

Only emergency operations were performed at weekends, so on Saturday morning very few staff were present in the department, the remainder being on call in case they were needed. It was a good time to make sure everything was up to date, and Rebecca Maine was in Theatre 1 cleaning and carrying out a stock check. 'Six Bard-Parker handles, four retractors, six spreaders . . .' she counted, ticking off the items listed on her clipboard.

Suddenly the doors swung open to admit Len McClure, distracting her for a second.

'Enjoy yourself last night, did you?' he said without preamble, pulling down the operating-table lights for inspection.

'Oh yes, Len, it was a good night – and thanks for the free drink, by the way. It was very generous of you.'

'Yes, a bit too generous, probably.' He laughed. 'Don't matter, though, so long as everybody enjoyed themselves. I know I did.' He began whistling, loudly and tunelessly, as he continued his examination of the theatre's machinery.

Rebecca suspended her count. It was impossible to concentrate in the face of the ODA's ear-piercing blast. 'Len, is the anaesthetic machine fixed now?'

'All sorted, Staff, you know me.'

'Oh yes, I know nothing gets past you, Len.'

'Absolutely, and not just the nuts-and-bolts stuff, either.' He winked conspiratorially. 'I'll tell you what, Staff. I've seen 'em come and go over the years here. We've had all sorts – and the goings-on to match,' he testified with a nod and raised eyebrows.

'Oh?' Her response was both inquisitive and uneasy. Had he somehow found out about her and Hugo? The hospital management frowned upon intra-departmental relationships at the best of times. They certainly wouldn't be impressed to discover that their star surgeon had been carrying on with his theatre nurse. Not to mention Hugo's wife, Jane, who worked part-time in the hospital's records department.

'Oh yeah,' Len continued. 'I couldn't repeat half the things

I've seen and heard. It's a real-life game of doctors and nurses round here sometimes.' He stopped what he was doing and stared at her. 'As I'm sure you're well aware, Staff.'

Rebecca felt her face reddening as she made her way to the scrub area. She and Hugo had done their level best to keep their affair under the radar, and so far as she knew they had been successful. If Len knew about it, then surely word would have spread throughout hospital by now. Len was no fool, though. He could just as easily be playing a mind game of his own. The surest way to get someone to give up their secrets was to pretend you already knew them. Well, two could play at that game. And flattery could get you everywhere.

'I'm sure I know almost nothing compared with you, Len,' she said. 'After all, I've only been on the staff for five minutes. I bet you've a few tales to tell, though, with all your years of experience. You're the oracle around here.'

'I suppose you could say that,' he said, visibly pleased. 'But I'm not one to gossip.'

'This wouldn't be gossip, just an exchange of information between professionals,' she said. 'Discretion is my middle name, Len,' she said.

'So I've heard,' he replied.

What did *that* mean? She decided to ignore it.

'So, doctors and nurses, eh? Anyone I know?' she probed.

Before he could answer, the wall phone rang. Rebecca walked across the room to answer it. 'Hello, Theatres? Yes, just a minute.' She flipped to the emergency list on her clipboard. Len made a drinking gesture and mouthed 'Tea?' She nodded and he left the room while she continued the call. 'Spinal trauma, right. At what time, please? OK, we'll be ready. Thanks.'

She replaced the handset, then lifted it again and made a series of calls to summon the members of the emergency team whose presence would be required.

Len returned bearing a tray on which were a pot of tea, two cups and a plate of digestives. 'What have we got, Staff?' he asked.

'A farmer whose tractor overturned. Nasty sounding spinal trauma. He's being transferred from Cirencester, arriving at one o'clock.'

'That's OK, then; we got time,' said Len. 'Everything in here is ready to go.'

'Anyway, Len, you were just about to share some of your secrets. I'm sure someone as sharp-eyed as you would know what goes on behind every door in this place.'

'Secrets? Too right. There are that many, I wouldn't know where to start.'

'Oh really?'

'Honest,' Len continued. 'I've seen all sorts over the years here. You nurses come and go. Broken relationships, affairs, you name it. Last November – the morning after Bonfire Night, it was – they found a student nurse in her room, dead. She'd hanged herself off the door hook. Suicide, they said, but I'm not so sure. There was no note, and nobody ever found out why she'd done it.'

Rebecca sipped her drink. 'So . . . what? Do you think she was, you know, bumped off or something?'

'Well, she was right as rain the night before, apparently. Went with her fiancé to the fireworks party they put on behind the social club and had a skinful, but she was found by the housekeeper first thing the following morning. We was all gobsmacked. Then a rumour went round that she'd had this massive row with her fella on the way home, but no one knew exactly what it was about. Just heard her saying she'd make sure everyone knew what he'd done. Perhaps it got a bit out of hand and he strangled her, then dressed the scene to make it look like she'd done herself in.'

'But there would have been evidence, wouldn't there? Forensics?' said Rebecca.

'Ah, but the fiancé was training to be a pathologist. He'd have known how to get round that. Picture the scene,' he added, clearly enjoying playing private detective. 'They get back to hers and she passes out, drunk. He decides he's had enough of her, chokes her with her own dressing-gown cord and hangs her up like an old raincoat. Job done!' Len assumed an I-rest-my-case expression and reached out for a biscuit.

'My God, that's awful!' said Rebecca, who thought that Len had clearly been watching too much *Quincey, ME.* 'So you definitely think the boyfriend did it?'

Len replied with a shrug. 'The post mortem said self-strangulation was the most likely cause of death and the coroner agreed. Lazy, if you ask me, jumping to the obvious conclusion like that. Doesn't matter what I think, though, does it? There was no evidence found at the scene, and the police weren't interested in listening to rumours.'

And I can guess who was trying to spread them, thought Rebecca.

'The bloke she was going out with didn't hang around for long afterwards, either,' continued Len. 'Took himself off to Malawi doing VSO. Still there, so far as I know.'

'You really are the fount of all knowledge, Len, aren't you?' she said.

'That's me, Staff,' said Len proudly.

'And what about now? Are there people still playing doctors and nurses?'

Len started at her for a moment, as if considering his words carefully. 'Well, I've got my suspicions that there's a certain party who's carrying on with one of the hospital's top brass. A married man.' He tapped the side of his nose. 'But if I told you, I'd have to kill you.'

'Just as well I'm a black belt in karate, then, isn't it?'

Len laughed uproariously, then stopped when he saw she wasn't smiling. 'Blimey, Staff, you're serious, aren't you?'

'Deadly serious, Len. I decided after my divorce that I wasn't going to get pushed around by anyone ever again.'

'Good for you, Staff; good for you,' he said admiringly. 'But I'm still not saying who's carrying on with who, even if you threaten me with the old kung-fu chop.'

He stood in a Bruce Lee pose and laughed again. Rebecca did her best to join in. He was clearly laughing at her rather than with her, but had his words been a joke or an insinuation?

'Waste of time, of course,' he added. 'Married men never leave their wives, in my experience.'

If that poison dart was aimed at her then it had missed its mark. The last thing Rebecca was looking for was a permanent relationship; that was why she preferred married men. An ill-starred marriage and an ugly divorce had left her with a jaundiced view of happy ever after. That said, she and Hugo were starting to see rather a lot of each other. If she were honest, this was becoming more than just a casual affair. No need to let Len in on her thoughts, though.

'You're right, Len. Some people never learn, do they?' agreed Rebecca.

Len frowned. Had he been expecting a different reaction, she wondered.

'Now . . . Sister Frazer,' he said.

'Go on,' said Rebecca, who had not missed Claire's brazen attempts to attract Hugo's attention the previous evening. She might only be Hugo's mistress, rather than his wife, but she certainly wasn't prepared to let someone as shallow as her take over that position without a fight. Then she realised Len was speaking not to her but over her shoulder. She turned to see Claire standing in the doorway.

'Hiya,' said Claire. 'Just to let you know we're all set next door for the spinal, when it arrives.'

'Great, thanks,' said Rebecca. 'We're good to go here, too.'

'There's one who's her own biggest fan,' said Len after Claire had left the room. 'Best-looking bird in the building – no offence, Staff – and a bloody good nurse too, but I wouldn't trust her no further than I could throw this table.'

'Why do you say that, Len?' asked Rebecca, but Len had already started his next yarn.

'This place is built on the site of a plague burial ground. I bet you didn't know that did you?' he said as he launched into a tale about the Grey Lady who floated through the hospital corridors at night. 'Every time she's seen, a patient dies the following day. It's said that she was . . .'

His voice morphed into white noise as Rebecca finished her tea, her thoughts haunted by more earthly concerns.

6

'So how do I look?' Claire did a twirl as she waited for Richie's verdict.

'You look like you always look, darling,' said Richie with a sigh. 'A million dollars. Now, can we get going? I told the chairman we'd be there by ten a.m. to welcome the clients.'

Both she and Richie were dressed in brand-new and very expensive Barbour waxed jackets that Richie had bought using his company credit card. She had insisted on a pair of skin-tight designer jeans, some rather nice ankle boots and a natty tweed cap to complete the ensemble. The occasion was the annual Harvest Sunday-morning clay-pigeon shoot organised by Richie's company, of which he was head of sales.

Richie was quite accomplished at the sport, but Claire had never held a gun in her life. Still, there were likely to be any number of well-off men attending. Who knew, she might even meet someone there who outshone Hugo. That would show Rebecca Maine!

'Claire? Are you ready?'

'Oh, sorry, Rich. I was miles away. Yes, come on, let's go.'

Claire pulled the front door shut behind her and looked up and down the street with a puzzled expression. 'Who's that parked in your usual space? I suppose you've had to leave the car miles away,' she grumbled. The spot where Richie habitually parked his Ford Sierra was now occupied by a much bigger vehicle she'd never seen before.

'Surprise!' said Richie. 'I've been promoted to assistant marketing director. This is my new company car. It's a Volvo 700 series.' He opened the passenger door for her. 'Turbocharged diesel engine, real leather seats . . .'

'Brilliant!' said Claire. 'There's a mirror in the sun visor so I can check my make-up when we get there.'

'Yes, that as well,' agreed Richie.

'Oh, Richie – look!' shouted Claire as they pulled away. 'Is that what I think it is?' She pointed to a rectangular block of plastic slotted into a holder on the dashboard. On it were buttons bearing numbers and symbols.

'Yep. They've given me a mobile phone so they can always

keep in touch. It's a Motorola. Top of the range.'

'But they cost hundreds of pounds, don't they?'

'A few thousand, actually,' said Richie.

'Wow! I'm impressed!'

Richie was clearly rising up the career ladder, and fast. Perhaps he might be worth hanging on to after all. Still, Hugo was already at the top, and so good looking . . .

***

'Got ya! And again, pull!' said Richie, annihilating his sixth successive clay. 'Your go.'

After some basic instruction from Richie, Claire got to have her turn. 'Ow!' she said, rubbing her shoulder as the stock of the 12-bore slammed into it.

'I warned you about the recoil, stupid,' said Richie. 'Keep it tight against your body.'

She missed with several attempts before finally hitting one.

'About time!' Richie said.

Claire glared at him and shouted 'Pull!' She fired again and again, clays exploding like fireworks in the cloudless sky. 'See what happens when I get angry? That'll teach you to call me stu—' the word died in her throat as she turned to see Richie pointing his gun straight at her with an iron-hard expression on his face.

'Richie? What the hell do you think you're doing! Even I know you should never point a loaded gun at someone!'

'Quite right too, young lady,' said a voice from behind her. 'Didn't they teach you anything at the gun club, Mr Evans?'

Richie's face split into a wide grin and Claire turned to find a well-dressed man in his seventies standing with a shotgun broken over his forearm.

'Claire, this is Charles Richards, the company chairman. It's his champagne we're enjoying today.'

'Pleased to meet you,' said Claire huffily. 'And thank you for inviting me, but I wish you could teach your employees how to behave.'

'Don't be silly, Claire,' said Richie. 'It's not loaded. I was just joking.'

'Well, I'm not laughing. Just because you're a big shot now . . .' she snapped.

'Don't you mean a big shotgun?' Richie teased.

Claire reddened and stormed off to the hospitality area, leaving her boyfriend and his boss to entertain their corporate clients.

'My, she's a lively one, isn't she?' she heard the older man say as she left.

Two hours and several glasses of red wine later, Richie came to find her.

'That was a great day all round, sweetheart,' he said, as though their spat had never happened. 'Got half a dozen new orders. Big ones, too. Have you been enjoying yourself?'

'Not as much as I thought I would,' Claire said with a pout. 'What's the matter, Richie? We never used to argue. Don't you like me being a good shot all of a sudden?'

'It's not about that.'

'What is it, then?'

'Nothing. Never mind. I've finished here now. Let's go for something to eat. There's a pub near here that serves food.'

Ten minutes later they pulled into the car park of Hunter's Lodge, a huge country-house inn nestling in green-belt splendour. The doors of the Volvo gently clicked shut behind

Claire as she stood and admired the view.

She had always liked country pubs, and Hunter's Lodge was a particularly attractive example. It had small-paned Georgian-style windows behind planters that still looked beautiful in the autumn sunlight, and two winding paths led to the front door, one from the car park and the other from the manicured outdoor seating area. Despite the building's bulk, it looked cosy and welcoming.

Richie walked round to take Claire's hand and lead her into the pub. 'What are you having?' he asked, taking his wallet from his inside pocket.

'I'd better just have an orange juice, I think. Your boss's wine has given me a headache.'

The pub was busy but not overcrowded. He ordered the drinks as soon as he caught the barman's eye, and they took them to a small table near the huge log fire. There were comfy sofas with thick cushions, fox-hunting scenes on the walls and an alcove with the owner's family tree painted on the wall. Although only a few people were still eating, the homely smell of Sunday roast lingered in the air. They both removed their jackets, made redundant by the fire's warmth.

'Claire, I've been thinking . . .' said Richie. As people chatted in the background, there was a raucous outburst of laughter from the bar. Richie paused, waiting for the volume to drop a little. 'I've been thinking,' he repeated. 'Why don't we go away for a break one weekend?'

Again the volume increased to almost drown his words. His timing wasn't quite right, but Claire caught their meaning. 'Where to?' she asked.

'Anywhere you like.'

'Nice idea. Let me think it over,' she said noncommittally. If they were going away, she'd be making the most of the opportunity and didn't want to waste it with an impulsive response. There were lots of nice places in England she could think of, but perhaps she should widen the net.

'What there is to think about?' said Richie, but he let it go with a slight puff of his cheeks, by now well accustomed to Claire's lack of enthusiasm.

The raucous customers left, and the atmosphere became a little quieter as he stood up to get another drink. 'Same again?'

he asked Claire.

'You won't get me drunk on orange juice, you know,' she said with a laugh.

'You can have something a bit stronger. It's me who's driving.'

'No, really, I'm fine, thanks.'

While Richie was at the bar, Claire reclined on the sofa, thinking.

'You look as though you're staying the night,' said Richie as he returned.

'Ha ha, you wish,' she said, sitting up. 'Although if I didn't have an early shift tomorrow, that wouldn't be a bad idea,' she added as she looked around at the luxurious surroundings.

They sipped their drinks in silence for a while, then Claire sidled up to Richie and put her hand on his knee. 'Darling, you know what you were saying earlier . . .' she said, stringing out the words. 'I was wondering. How about a weekend in Paris?' She put her arm round his shoulder.

'At last, a spark of romance!' he exclaimed. 'Hey, everybody, the drinks are on me!'

'Shh! OK, calm down.'

'No, Claire, I might just have to have a lie down to recover!' he said, trying to ease himself out of her grip. 'Hold on, are you sure you're all right?' he added, placing his hand on her forehead.

'Richie, I'm warning you. I'll change my mind if you keep on.'

They both ended up laughing, their earlier disagreement forgotten.

'Are you hungry?' he asked.

'Not really,' said Claire.

'Me neither. OK, come on, then, drink up.'

'Where to now?'

'Anywhere. Let's just go for a spin in the new motor.'

They thanked the barman on the way out and headed off in the Volvo, further into the countryside. The low sunlight streamed through the trees, bathing the interior in shades of green and gold. Claire picked a CD from the car's storage rack and the cabin filled with music as they drove on, enjoying the scenery.

Claire jumped as a noisy vibration filled the air.

'What's that? Is the engine broken?'

'Relax,' said Richie, picking up the mobile. 'It's just the phone. Hello? Oh hi!' he said. 'Yes, she's here. I'll hand you over.' He looked at Claire with a smile. 'It's for you.'

'For me?' Claire took the mobile excitedly. 'Hello? Who's this? . . . Jinny! How did you get Richie's number? . . . Oh, I see . . . Yes, the new car *was* a surprise. I'm amazed you could keep the secret . . . Mmm, we've had a lovely day from start to finish, thanks.'

Richie shot her a sideways glance.

'And guess what? We're going to Paris! . . . I know, it's brilliant, isn't it? . . . OK, I'll see you at work tomorrow. Bye. Bye.'

She replaced the phone in its cradle. 'My first mobile phone call! You arranged that with Jinny so that I could feel special, didn't you? Thanks. That was thoughtful.'

'We aim to please, madam,' said Richie. Then, more seriously, 'I do love you, Claire, you know.'

As if by unspoken agreement, they drove into a secluded

lane, turned the music down and began to 'christen the new car' as Richie put it. Then Claire spotted movement in the bushes ahead and a man and his dog appeared.

She pushed Richie's mouth away from her breast, frantically pulling her clothing over her uncovered flesh, her face like thunder as the stranger delighted in the unexpected peep show.

He laughed as he walked slowly by. 'You ought to sell tickets,' he said. 'You'd make a fortune.'

Richie started the engine and shouted out the window, 'Piss off, you pervert, or get run over.' The shock of their unexpected exposure had unsettled both of them. Richie put the car into gear and drove back through the winding lanes at speed, mounting verges and negotiating hairpin bends on two wheels. *He really does drive like a maniac at times*, thought Claire as she sat back and enjoyed the ride.

7

At 8.30 on Monday morning Jane Bowman was just about to sit down to breakfast when the phone rang. It was Tim Dawson, Hugo's registrar.

'Hi, Jane. Is Hugo there?'

'He's out on his morning run, Tim. Can I give him a message?'

'If you wouldn't mind, Jane. Could you tell him we've got a total hip for the list this afternoon, please? I warn you, though, he isn't going to be happy.'

'I'll hide all the sharp implements when I tell him then, shall I?' said Jane. 'Thanks for the heads-up.'

Tim laughed. 'I don't think you need to go that far. Besides, he sees enough sharp objects at work. Just tell him it's Simon's fault. He's our new house officer,' he explained.

They chatted for a while and as she replaced the receiver Jane reflected what a nice man Tim was. Whenever she saw him he had a smile on his face, unlike her husband, who seemed increasingly distracted and irascible of late. She worried that their marriage was in danger of becoming one of convenience: he brought home the bacon and she cooked it for him. Sometimes she felt more like her husband's housekeeper than his wife, or even less than that. At least if she'd been a housemaid he might have made a pass at her. She couldn't recall the last time they'd made love.

Jane was drying her cereal bowl as Hugo returned, glowing from his exercise, and plonked down his morning paper onto the breakfast bar.

'Tim rang while you were out,' she said as he headed for the shower. 'Apparently you've got a total hip to do this afternoon.'

Hugo stopped in his tracks. 'What! Whose idea idea was that? He should know total hip replacements need to be on the morning list.'

'He said to blame Simon,' replied Jane.

'Simon! I might have guessed. I wish he'd think about what he's doing. I'll be working half the night now. I'm up at the Lavender Clinic for some private work later,' he said. 'Keep you in the style to which you've become accustomed, eh?'

After showering, Hugo returned to the lounge, where he unfolded his *Financial Times* and scanned the latest share prices while sipping filtered coffee. Jane sat in her recliner, leafing through her diary, hoping to discover that something interesting might be on the horizon but finding instead only dates for upcoming beauty treatments and hairdressing appointments. She looked over at her husband. *He wouldn't even notice if I dyed my hair purple*, she thought as she glared at him resentfully.

The 'style to which she had become accustomed' was an exquisite six-bedroomed house in Springfields, a newly built executive development three miles from Harvington town centre. Its furnishings were luxurious, its decor unblemished, its appointments exquisite. Yet for Jane it had no soul. It was as sterile as a film set.

'What time are you in?' she asked, hoping they might take a walk together before he left.

'Any time now,' said Hugo as he checked his wristwatch, finished his last drop of coffee and stood to leave.

'Actually, Hue, I was wondering . . .'

'Not now, please, Jane,' he said. 'I really don't have time to chat.'

She wondered why it was always she who had to make the effort. He was there in body, but it felt as though his mind was always somewhere else. She felt a surge of anger. How could he be so nonchalant? The feelings overwhelmed her.

Hugo was in the hallway, knotting his tie in front of the Ettore Sottsass mirror that hung there. She swiftly rose from the recliner, walked to the lounge door and vented her feelings with barely suppressed rage. She wanted to explode, but instead she attacked him with an acid tongue.

'Has anyone ever told you how much of a jumped-up bastard you can be at times?' she said, standing with her hands on her hips.

'Only you, dear,' he said calmly. 'I'll be finishing late, so don't bother leaving me a meal.'

Jane stood watching from the window as he reversed out of the drive. Their twenty-five years of marriage had been spent building Hugo's career and raising their two children, both now at university. There was no financial reason for her to work, but her part-time post in the hospital's records department helped to fill the emptiness she felt from a moribund marriage and an empty nest. Jane's eyes glazed with tears as she recalled the almost unconditional love they had once felt for each other. Once in a starring role as wife and mother, she was now little more than a scene-shifter on her husband's stage.

She reflected how lucky she was to have Claire Frazer in her life. The pair had recently sat next to each other at an internal staff training course and they had hit it off straight away. Claire was kind and so understanding – a breath of fresh air – and only too willing to provide a sympathetic ear for Jane's marital woes. Jane did not have many friends she felt she could trust, but who better than Hugo's lead nurse to help her get her marriage back on track? Hugo had no idea they'd formed a friendship and Claire had advised her not to mention it to him, in case he became more guarded at work. That made sense to Jane. It was a comfort to know that she had an ally in the enemy camp.

A sudden knock at the back door interrupted her thoughts.

She opened it to find Jeff Glass, their appropriately named window cleaner, on the step. His van was in the drive, *Glass the Glass*, signwritten on the side above his telephone number and logo – a dragon holding a bucket and ladder.

'Morning, Mrs B. I'll just carry on, then, is it?' he asked, his usual Welsh sing-song voice monotonic and his shoulders slumped as if he just wanted to get the job over and done with. That was unusual for Jeff, who was normally full of beans.

'Yes, that's fine, Jeff. There'll be a coffee waiting for you when you're done.'

Once the percolator was bubbling, she went to the en-suite bathroom of the bedroom she and Hugo shared. The full blast of the power shower pummelled her body, refreshing and reviving her mind and helping to relax her inner angst. After drying herself, and wearing only a turban fashioned from the towel, she flitted in and out of their bedroom, fetching items of make-up and her hair dryer. With everything to hand, she began massaging body lotion into her thighs one at a time, using a chair as a footstool, then stood drying her hair, her mind on other things and completely oblivious of the outside world.

As she returned to the en-suite and began applying her make-up, she became aware of a squeaking noise coming from the bedroom. With a shock, she recognised the sound of chamois leather on glass. Jeff! She'd completely forgotten about him. Had he been watching through the window as she'd paraded around stark naked?

The thought should have mortified her, but she was surprised to find that she found the idea rather erotic. Jeff was a good-looking guy, younger than her by ten years, with a Colgate smile and the look of Richard Gere. None the less, these were hardly thoughts that a married woman approaching middle age should be entertaining. She could feel her face reddening with embarrassment.

Jane plucked up courage and went downstairs to pour coffees, leaving one on the side for Jeff, who was now working at ground level. She opened the kitchen window. 'Jeff, will you be long?' she called out awkwardly. 'I've got to go to work, and I'll need to lock up.'

'I'm only half done, Mrs B,' he replied, 'but to be honest

I'm not feeling too clever today. Dodgy chow mein last night I think it was, and it looks like rain anyway. Tell you what, how about if I come round and redo the lot for you on Wednesday?'

For the next ten minutes he stood in the doorway drinking his coffee, spouting chapter and verse about the effects of unpredictable weather on a window cleaner's trade. It looked as though Jane had managed to get away with her accidental strip show – or was Jeff simply being diplomatic? Something seemed to have cheered him up, anyway, she reflected. She offered him a five-pound note but he waved it away and departed with a friendly 'Pay me on Wednesday.'

Despite what she had told Jeff, Jane didn't work on Mondays, and as she contemplated how she would fill the day she felt a sudden urge to phone Celia, her best and oldest friend but one she had neglected lately.

The ringing continued for a few seconds, and then, 'Hello?'

'Celia, it's me, Jane.'

'Oh hi, darling . . . how lovely to hear from you at long last. Has something terrible happened?' Celia could be a little sarcastic at times, not to mention rather dramatic.

'No, nothing has happened . . . well, nothing terrible, but I think I might have been caught in an embarrassing situation.'

'Oh, Jane, I'm intrigued. What on earth have you been up to?'

'Well, it's like this: I was in my bedroom with nothing on, putting cream on my legs, and I completely forgot that the window cleaner was here, and . . . and, well, I'm not sure if he saw me.' Jane could hardly spit the words out for breaking into a hysterical giggle.

'What? You mean . . . No, surely not!' Celia's voice began to crack. 'Are you telling me he caught you in the nude?'

'Well, that's just it. I don't know. And, if he did, then I'm not sure how I feel about it.'

'My God, what is the matter with you, love? You don't seem to know whether you're coming or going.'

Jane imagined Celia's expressive face contorting with every twist of emotion. Although in her mid-fifties, Celia was one of the most beautiful women Jane had ever seen, with deep coffee-coloured skin that declared her Caribbean heritage and black bobbed hair that shone like obsidian. She was always impeccably dressed.

Celia continued. 'You're not with it, are you? I'm not sure whether to split my sides or call the doctor to you, girl.' Then she broke into a most infectious laugh that seem to recycle itself uncontrollably. Jane knew it would be pointless trying to get any more words in edgeways until it stopped.

'Have you quite finished?' asked Jane when the noise subsided.

Celia tried hard to suppress a giggle. 'Listen, what are you doing this afternoon?'

'Not a lot,' said Jane. 'I never am.'

'OK, in that case, why not come over for lunch?'

'Mm, that's seems like a good idea, Celia.'

'Smashing! I'll see you at one o'clock, then, and we'll have a good old catch-up.'

Jane replaced the receiver, pleased that she could rely on her friends, at least.

8

Hugo parked his royal blue Mercedes in his reserved space and entered the main building, deep in thought about the complex operation he was about to undertake. As he turned the corner, he collided with Claire, causing her to drop a set of medical notes.

'Sister Frazer, I'm so sorry!' he said, his eyes drawn inexorably to her cleavage as she knelt to retrieve the paperwork.

He bent down to help just as she rose to her feet, catching him in the face with her head.

'Ouch!' he said, rubbing his nose. 'That'll teach me, won't it?'

'Oh dear, are you all right, Mr Bowman?' said Claire.

'I don't think it's broken,' he said. 'And anyway, if it is, then I'm in the right place, aren't I?'

They laughingly exchanged more pained apologies. Then their eyes met and the laughter ceased, with each momentarily lost in the other's gaze.

Hugo had been attracted to his lead nurse from the moment he saw her. So attracted, in fact, that he had almost broken his cardinal first rule of extramarital affairs: don't get involved if there's a partner. He had introduced the maxim after receiving a rather violent comeuppance from a receptionist's Royal Marine husband five years ago, a chastisement the pain in his nose was now reminding him of. Still, Clare Frazer was a sight to behold, and that chap she was with was only a salesman or something, wasn't he? Perhaps this would be a rule worth breaking for once. And she'd made it clear at the social club that she'd be interested.

'Sister Frazer. Claire. May I call you Claire? I wonder whether –'

Suddenly, they were distracted by Hugo's name being called loudly from down the corridor. It was Rebecca Maine, requesting his presence in theatre. Hugo looked round guiltily. Len McClure, of all people, was standing next to his theatre staff nurse. It had to be Len, the hospital gossip. Had he overheard the exchange between him and Claire? Had

81

Rebecca?'

'I'll be there directly, Staff. Just helping Sister Frazer get her notes in order,' he explained. He turned back to Claire. 'As I was saying, Sister,' he said, loudly enough for Len and Rebecca to hear. 'I wonder whether you would keep a personal eye on my total hip when I've finished with him. It's a major operation and he'll need the best care during recovery.'

'Of course, Mr Bowman,' said Claire, and turned to leave.

Hugo watched her go. Was it his imagination or were those hips swinging a little more freely than usual?

Hugo shook his head to clear it and went to the locker room, emerging ten minutes later in green surgical overalls. He met Tim in the medical room after rechecking the morning's orthopaedic schedule. They discussed the day's list and then Rebecca helped them to scrub up.

Thirty minutes into the total hip replacement one of the overhead lights began to flicker. 'Len, lights please!' As Len activated the backup lighting unit, Hugo concentrated intensely, targeting questions at the main players involved in the case. 'Blood pressure, Danny?'

His question was directed at a rangy, long-haired man in his mid-thirties, who looked as though he would be more at home playing lead guitar in a rock group than keeping patients sedated, but Danny Edwards was one of the best anaesthetists Hugo had ever worked with, and he was delighted to have him on the surgical team. Danny reassured Hugo that all was well.

'Let me see the pictures, Staff.'

Immediately, Rebecca Maine placed a series X-rays up on the light box showing the operation site from every angle.

It was a long procedure, with the atmosphere sometimes tense as alarm warnings sounded on the anaesthetic equipment, but Danny had everything under control and Hugo couldn't help but smile beneath his mask as the younger man assured the worried junior assistants, 'It's cool, man. Just chill.'

An hour and a half later the operation was complete and Danny began to reverse the effects of the anaesthetic. Hugo stretched, arching his back, and removed his latex gloves. His smiling eyes could be seen above his mask.

'Thank you all,' he said, nodding with appreciation. Hugo shook Danny's hand as well as Len's.

'Always a pleasure to work with someone who operates as smooth as yourself, sir, if you get my drift,' said the ODA. Did Len really wink as he said that or was Hugo just imagining it?

The theatre staff competed to undo the ties on his gown from behind as though it was a privilege, and indeed it was for many. Rebecca Maine, whom he would later be taking to dinner before, he hoped, they embarked on a very different sort of horizontal procedure, handed the notes to Hugo with a whispered 'See you later.' He left the theatre, clomping down the corridor in his clogs towards the medical room to write them up.

***

While Harvington's star surgeon had been working his magic, Claire had been sitting in the recovery room, quietly thinking, her arms folded on the desk. Libby pottered around in silence for a time, observing her curiously.

'Are you OK?' asked Libby, with half a grin and eyebrows scrunched together.

'Mm, yes,' answered Claire.

'Your face is a dead giveaway, if you don't mind me saying,'

Libby replied.

'No, I'm fine,' Claire insisted, though the truth was, she was all in a dither.

All three theatres were in use that morning, and the recovery room was running well, with so far no complications. 'Back in a mo,' Claire said, and walked over to see Jinny in the department clerk's office as a perplexed Libby watched her leave.

Jinny looked up from the file she was reading as Claire plonked herself down on a corner of her desk. 'What's the matter?' she asked. 'You look like someone with a problem.'

'I feel as if I've got snakes in my stomach,' Claire said with a pathetic grin.

Without rising, Jinny wheeled her office chair round to face her friend. 'You have what? Did you say snakes?'

'Yeah, you know,' continued Claire, rubbing her stomach. 'Oh, all right, butterflies, then, but it's worse than that.' She lowered her voice. 'You know I told you last week how I feel about Hugo?'

'Yes, and I told you to think about what you've got before

you throw it away!' said Jinny.

'I know, I know,' said Claire brushing aside the objection. 'But this morning I think we had a moment.'

'What do you mean, "a moment"?'

'Well, earlier on we bumped into each other –'

'That's hardly unusual in a hospital,' Jinny interrupted.

'No, I mean *literally* bumped into each other. And then I banged him on the nose with my head and we both started laughing and –'

'What? This sounds more like a boxing match than a "moment".'

'Shh. Let me finish, will you? He picked up some notes I'd dropped, and as he handed them back to me our eyes met and – I don't know, Jinny, but I'm sure there was something there between us.'

'Hmm, that sounds a little bit like wishful thinking to me, Claire. Did he say anything?'

'Yes. No. Actually, I think perhaps he was going to ask me out, but then we were interrupted by Rebecca Maine.'

'Ah,' said Jinny, in a that-explains-it voice.

'Is he really seeing her, do you think, Jin?'

'Oh, I don't know. You know what this place is like for gossip. It could all be just hot air.'

They both turned towards the door as the bell rang at the transfer bay to announce the arrival of another patient to the department.

'Come over tonight and we can talk about it properly,' said Claire. 'That will be Hugo's total hip. I'd better go back. I've left Libby in charge but I promised Hugo I'd take care of this one personally.'

'He must at least admire your nursing skills, then,' said Jinny.

'I'd sooner he admired something else,' said Claire with a wink.

'You're playing with fire, you know,' warned Jinny, but Claire had already left.

Claire returned to the recovery room just as Hugo's patient arrived. As soon as the man was fully awake, and she was satisfied that he would suffer no complications, she asked Lyn Hawes to arrange his return to the ward and walked over to the medical room, where she knew Hugo would be writing up his notes. She gave him a brief progress report and offered him a coffee as she made one for herself. He accepted with a pleasant smile as she placed the cup within his reach, and once again their eyes locked.

Claire felt as though she was falling into two blue pools that somehow seemed constantly to vary in shade and depth. At least, it seemed that way. She longed to run her fingers through his thick blond hair.

The metallic rattling of a trolley in the distance broke their stare, and she released the cup handle, suggesting she would return for the notes a little later.

'That's fine,' he said. 'I'll bring them in if you like.'

'I'll look forward to it,' she said.

As she turned to leave the room, Rebecca Maine appeared, straightening her theatre tunic as though she was about to rip it completely off had she pulled much harder. She looked like a lioness, angry to find a challenger on her territory, and she stared at the coffee cup as if it had just materialized from thin air.

It was an unwritten rule of the hospital that the theatre staff nurse always saw to the needs of the head surgeon. It was part of the job's kudos, and Rebecca was clearly unhappy that Claire had usurped her. Now, with a face like thunder, as if someone had kicked a pedestal from under her, she helped herself to a drink as if doing so was an experience more painful than childbirth. She leaned against the windowsill with a solemn stare aimed at Claire, who was grinning from ear to ear as she turned and made her way back to the recovery room.

9

It was now one o'clock, and Claire organised the lunch breaks with her staff while she and Libby continued to monitor a knee-replacement recovery. Then Hugo walked in with the notes, bestowing upon the room a gorgeous smile that she wished has been for her benefit alone.

'I think I trod on somebody's toes earlier,' she commented.

'Staff Nurse Maine, you mean? Really, I shouldn't worry about it. She acts like a mother hen around me at times,' he reassured her offhandedly, still smiling. That was hardly leaping to her rival's defence, was it? Perhaps Jinny had got the wrong end of the stick, and there was nothing going on between them after all. He hadn't even called Rebecca by her first name.

Claire was sure that, like all men, Hugo lapped up attention from women, even though he was married. Meeting Jane Bowman at that training session had been a stroke of luck, she reflected. Jane had been only too keen to divulge her marital problems. She'd even followed Claire's advice not to tell Hugo they were friends, which suited Claire's purposes admirably, for she doubted that even Hugo would be cavalier enough to date his wife's good friend. Clearly, the Bowmans' was not a happy home. Was it unhappy enough for Hugo to begin an affair with his theatre nurse, though? In one sense, she hoped Jinny was right, because it would mean he was persuadable. Either way, it made no difference to her feelings. She was absolutely infatuated with him.

'Everything all right with my total hip?' he asked, nodding at the client.

'But of course,' she said. 'Personal service, as requested. We're just waiting for the nod from Kingfisher Ward to send him back up.'

Len walked past, wheeling an empty oxygen cylinder to the transfer bay pick-up point, turning his head to stare at Hugo and Claire as they bent over the notes. They both looked up as he began to whistle a song Claire recognised, but couldn't name, acknowledging them with a wave as he made his way back to the medical room.

Hugo straightened up and stepped back a pace. 'Hang on, Len!' he called out. 'I need a word about those operating lights.'

Len looked up. 'No problem, sir. I'll be in the theatre when you're ready.'

'Good afternoon, Staff Nurse Hancock,' Hugo said, as Libby walked up to them. 'Thank you, Sister Frazer, and, as I said, pay no attention to the mother hen.'

Libby was intrigued. 'What was he on about?'

'Oh, I was referring to the way Rebecca Maine was acting earlier on,' Claire answered. 'All I did was make his coffee,' she added, shrugging her shoulders.

Libby mimicked a pained expression. 'Oh dear, hands caught in the cookie jar?'

'I didn't even see any biscuits in there,' said Claire, who could take things a little too literally at times. 'Anyway, I didn't think it was a crime.'

'Dearie me,' continued Libby. 'Life can't possibly go on if someone else makes the great man his coffee. Really? . . . I ask you.'

'Exactly,' said Claire, pleased at Libby's sarcasm. 'Welcome to the Rebecca Maine nursery for middle-aged spinsters.'

'Ooh, now now, Claire,' Libby replied with a grin. 'To be fair, she's divorced, and only thirty-six, but I know what you mean. She can get a bit territorial.'

Claire asked Libby to chase up Kingfisher Ward's bed manager and signed off another successful recovery report. The staff on first lunch had returned. Among them was Amanda Stoles, the department's first-year student. She was chatting to Karen Thomas, another student, now in her second year of training. Karen had done a stint in the recovery unit during her first year and was now on a six-month theatre rotation. A mousy little thing, and someone Claire always thought seemed scared of her own shadow, she had nevertheless left a good impression on the permanent recovery room staff as a nurse who could be trusted to do her job with the minimum of supervision.

'Hi, Karen, how are you?' asked Claire.

'Fine, thank you, Sister Frazer,' Karen replied with a smile and little eye contact. 'I've just come for Mr Bowman's notes. Only if you've finished with them, of course.' Her nervous disposition clearly hadn't improved under Rebecca Maine's tutelage.

As Karen took the file from her, Claire noticed that her fingernails, bitten halfway down the nail beds, betrayed the full extent of her inner conflict.

'I do feel sorry for Karen,' she muttered to Libby as the young girl walked away.

'I know,' said Libby. 'It's a shame, isn't it, the pressure these kids are under. You need to be tough to survive in this profession.'

'And hungry to succeed,' added Claire.

'Speaking of which, I'm off to lunch,' announced Libby.

'Hang on, wait for me,' said Claire. 'I've brought sandwiches too today.'

As they walked towards the staff room they passed Jinny in her office, tucking into her sandwiches while reading the paper. Claire and Libby turned to each other outside the office door and sniffed the air.

'Egg!' they both said at once, laughing loudly.

Jinny looked up from her paper wearing a puzzled

expression as Claire and Libby tried to straighten their faces.

'Don't forget you're coming over tonight, Jinny,' said Claire.

Jinny, her mouth full, gave her the thumbs-up. 'No worries,' she said after swallowing the last of her sandwich, much to the relief of everyone around her. The smell was noisome.

'"No worries"?' said Libby, as they continued down the corridor to the staff room. 'I thought only Australians said that.'

'Jinny's a big fan of *Neighbours*,' explained Claire.

As she and Libby sat unwrapping their packed lunches, the sound of raised voices in the corridor suddenly disturbed the usually tranquil ambience of the theatre department. Claire and Libby exchanged glances, frowning as the row seemed to get worse and nearer. They opened the door to reveal an ongoing altercation in the corridor between Rebecca Maine and Iain Stewart, the assistant ODA.

'If I say I want it done like that, then you'll do it like that!' shouted Rebecca.

'Ah take my instructions from Mr McClure, no' some jumped-up bedpan washer,' retorted Iain, a Glaswegian whose temper was as fiery as his ginger hair.

Within minutes there was a crossfire of verbal lashings as Eddy, one of the theatre porters, stepped in to defend Rebecca's honour while Len weighed in to protect his protégé.

Tension was in the air – you could cut it with a knife.

Claire abandoned her lunch and strode down the corridor in full Valkyrie mode.

'What on earth do you think you're doing?' she asked in a fierce whisper. 'This is a hospital, not a playground! I'm the lead nurse in this department, and once you come through those theatre doors you all take your instructions from me! There are patients here trying to recover. The last thing they need to hear is some sort of Western brawl going on.'

Rebecca shot Claire a dagger-filled glance and stormed back into theatre while the three men stood staring at their shoes like naughty schoolboys as they absorbed her tirade.

'Don't ever let me see this sort of thing again,' she added before returning to her lunch, a stunned Libby trailing in her wake.

Lyn Hawes entered the staff room with a serious expression and raised eyebrows to go with her Pot Noodle.

'Any idea what that was all about?' asked Claire.

'Yes,' said Lyn, who usually had her ear to the ground. 'Apparently, Staff had been on at him, picking holes in his work.'

Claire looked puzzled 'Who, Iain? How strange. He's the last person I'd have thought needed a dressing down. He's almost as good at the job as Len.'

Lyn sighed as she shifted papers on the desk. 'Everyone in theatre is saying she has a vile mood on her at the moment.'

Claire hadn't calmed down entirely just yet. 'Well I'm disgusted! Surely they could have taken it to the theatre. It was empty, after all.' Claire couldn't finish her lunch; she was too annoyed, and still pumped full of adrenalin from the encounter. Lyn and Libby decided it would be safer to leave her to it and returned to the recovery room.

Shortly after they had left, Jinny popped her head round the door. 'What the hell did you say up there? Nobody wants to breathe . . . except your patients, of course,' she added quickly as she realised her faux pas. 'Is it OK to come in, or will you bite my head off too?' she asked sheepishly.

'Do you have to be so dopey all the time, Jinny?' snapped Claire, who was still simmering and didn't look at all impressed. 'Try one of the other six dwarves for a change.'

Jinny's smile slowly evaporated. 'O-kay,' she said slowly as she slithered back behind the door to return to her office.

'Jinny, wait!' called Claire, hurrying out of the room to catch her up. 'I'm sorry, I didn't mean that. You're still coming round tonight, aren't you? I need someone to talk to.'

'Oh, I'm not too dopey for that, then?' she said sternly, then smiled and punched Claire's arm playfully. 'Of course I am, you fool. I know you're only annoyed because you care about your patients.'

'Among other things,' said Claire.

'What do you –'

'Never mind. We'll talk tonight. Eight o'clock sharp,' said Claire. 'Bring wine.'

The rest of the afternoon passed peacefully, with only two

small procedures: an ingrown toenail and a Colles' fracture of the forearm. Claire decided to let Libby and Lyn leave early and asked Amanda to help Paula, her second SEN, to restock and do some damp dusting.

The last two cases were as uncomplicated as she had anticipated, which enabled the rest of the staff to leave on time. Claire penned in the names of those on call for the evening in case of emergency, then picked up her bag and left the building.

The air was cool and refreshing against her face and she breathed in deeply, relieved to get away from those clinically cold walls that left her feeling drained after an eight-hour shift. She walked slowly at first, letting the day fall from her shoulders, then quickened her step towards her Mini Cooper and started the engine.

On the radio was playing the song that Len had been whistling earlier. Now that she could hear the words, she recognised it immediately.

'There's a golden oldie from the fifties for you,' said the DJ as the music finished. 'Hank Williams with "Your Cheatin'

Heart".'

10

It was six thirty by the time Claire arrived home. She flung her car keys on the hall table, slid a chicken-and-vegetable pie in the oven and set the timer for thirty minutes before removing her coat. She filled a tumbler with ice-cold milk from the fridge and took a mouthful, then stood holding the glass to her chest, replaying in her mind the way Hugo had looked at her in the corridor just hours ago. Suddenly the phone rang, making her jump. On the line was Jane Bowman.

'Oh, hi, Jane! How are you?' she asked, feeling as though she had been caught red handed. She was finding it increasingly difficult to maintain the facade of being a loyal friend to a woman whose husband she intended to steal. Nevertheless, she did genuinely enjoy Jane's company, and the insight she might gain into her quarry's personality could prove invaluable.

'I'm at home and bored witless,' replied Jane.

'I take it Hugo's not back yet,' said Claire.

'You've got to be joking. He's up at the Lavender Clinic. Or so he says.'

What did she mean by that? Jane had confided that Hugo seemed increasingly distant of late, but if she was now suspecting an actual affair, Claire would have to watch her step even more carefully.

'Oh, right. Yes, I do think he said something about an evening appointment there,' said Claire, who could recall nothing of the kind. Damn! With Hugo out and about, this would have been the perfect opportunity to have Jane come over for a confidential chat, if only she hadn't already asked Jinny. 'I'm sure he'll be home before long,' she added. 'Anyway, what have you been up to?'

'Nothing much. My days off are hardly action packed,' said Jane.

Was it Claire's imagination, or was Jane slurring her words slightly? That 'action' had sounded suspiciously sibilant. It was a bit early in the evening to be tipsy, even for Claire.

'Although, actually, I did do something today; I had lunch bought for me by an old friend, Celia, which was nice of her, and then we both had our nails done.'

'There you are, then,' said Claire. In the kitchen, her oven timer began to bleep. 'Look, I'm sorry to be rude, Jane, but can I catch up with you another time? I'm meeting Jinny this evening and I need to get changed.'

'I'm glad at least one of us has got a social life,' said Jane glumly, hanging up before Claire could answer.

She left her pie on the kitchen worktop to cool while she took a shower. Ten minutes later she returned in a thick white bathrobe, her hair in a towelling turban, and ate her dinner from a tray on her lap while she watched TV.

The weather had turned much cooler in the week since Jinny's last visit, and tonight she dressed in casual jeans and a large white sloppy joe jumper. Restless as she awaited Jinny's arrival, she poured herself a brandy. Just as she swirled the last drop from the bulbous glass around in her mouth, the doorbell rang. Her cheeks inflated before she swallowed as if she had just rinsed with mouthwash.

'So, c'mon then,' said Jinny as she entered the living room, parking her bag by the armchair. 'What's been going on?'

'Hold your horses. Did you bring wine?'

'I, er, no. I didn't have time to call at the off-licence. I'm sorry.'

'Not to worry, I've got some in. Let's get a bottle opened,' suggested Claire. She filled two glasses and grabbed a bag of peanuts to take to the living room. 'Right, that's better,' she said as she slumped into the soft leather of the sofa. 'Now, then. Hugo. I think there's really a chance I can get him into bed.'

The shock wiped the smile off Jinny's face. 'No, Claire, that's just wrong! I told you, not only is he married, I think he's also seeing Rebecca Maine.'

'After the way she was behaving today, I'm *sure* he's seeing her,' Claire said. 'But I just can't help it.' She shrugged her shoulders with raised eyebrows and chewed her bottom lip, hoping her best friend would not think any the less of her.

'And if he's the sort to cheat on both his wife *and* his mistress, what makes you think he won't two-time you?' said Jinny.

'Well, I'm better looking than both of them for a start,' said

Claire.

'Oh, Claire, I know you're my best friend, but you can be absolutely self-destructive at times. You do worry me.'

'Where's your sense of humour gone?' said Claire. 'I know it's not just about looks, Jinny. I'm not that shallow.'

Jinny raised her eyebrows but kept her own counsel.

'We're right for each other, I know it,' Claire continued. 'If we were together, he wouldn't look at anyone else. Besides, I'm sure his wife's an alcoholic,' she added, blithely taking a large swig from her wine glass.

'And what about Richie?' Jinny asked.

'Well, that's another problem, because he wants us both to go away for a weekend. Actually, I asked him to take me to Paris, but after today I'm not sure I want to go anywhere with anyone except Hugo.'

'So, what are you going to do?'

'It's a bind, isn't it?' Claire took another gulp of red wine. 'Come on, drink up! You've hardly touched yours.'

Jinny ignored her. 'Does Hugo definitely like you, Claire? Are you certain?'

'Oh, I know he does; I can tell,' said Claire, utterly sure of herself.

'Well!' said Jinny. 'You don't half take some chances, I must say.'

'I'm a woman on a mission,' Claire countered as she refilled her glass and made to top up Jinny's.

'No, I've got the car tonight,' Jinny protested. 'And . . .'

'And what?' said Claire.

'Well, Claire, I have a secret of my own. No one else knows, other than Brian. Not a soul.'

Claire looked at Jinny's full glass again. 'You're not?' she said. 'You're not, are you? Jinny, are you really?'

'I am! Yes, I'm pregnant, Claire.' Jinny made the confirmation with such pride that for a moment Claire was slightly jealous, even though being pregnant was the last condition she wanted to find herself in. But they still hugged and squealed with joy, jumping up and down, pausing for breath, and then doing it again, waving their arms hysterically.

'Shh, though,' said Jinny with a broad smile, obviously pleased with Claire's response. 'Just don't you dare say anything. I mean it!'

Claire, who by now had managed to calm herself, made the promise. Still fizzing with excitement, she asked how Brian had taken the news.

'He's over the moon, of course, but he doesn't want me to say anything to anyone at work yet. He says it's bad luck. He said it would be OK to tell you and Richie, but no one else.'

'Do you know how far gone you are?' asked Claire.

'Not exactly, but we did one of those home-testing kits last night, and the reaction was virtually immediate.' She stated rubbing her tummy as if desperate to start showing.

'Gosh, you kept that quiet!'

'Like I said, we weren't going to tell anyone just yet, but . . . well, tonight seemed like an occasion for sharing secrets.'

'Jinny, I am so pleased for you both,' said Claire, surprised to find that she meant the words sincerely.

'Thank you,' Jinny said proudly. 'And you'll be godmother, of course.'

Claire doubted she was an ideal role model for any child,

but decided not to prick her friend's bubble by saying so.

'So how late were you when you did the test?' she asked instead.

'Just over three weeks. You know I'm never late.'

'Mm, that's true. You're about the most regular in the department.'

Jinny agreed. 'Isn't it funny how the monthly cycles of women working together for a long time automatically begin to synchronise?'

'Absolutely, there is supposedly scientific evidence,' agreed Claire, wondering as the conversation continued how on earth the subject had changed from her love life to inexplicable phenomena in human biology. Although perhaps they weren't so different after all.

11

Jane Bowman was busy helping herself to drinks from the bar in the corner of the lounge. It was always well stocked, though only occasionally used, but this evening she had decided it had been neglected for far too long, and was making up for lost time. Things had gotten to her. She was not only becoming increasingly uneasy about Hugo and his ever-more frequent absences while 'working late' but also concerned that she hadn't heard much from her friend Claire Frazer recently. Claire was a good listener and Jane was anxious to ask her opinion about what she feared was her failing marriage. Over lunch, Celia had just told her not to worry, but she didn't know Hugo as well as Claire did. Jane had hoped for an invitation to meet when she had rung Claire earlier, but her friend didn't seem to be able to get off the phone fast enough. She consoled herself that she must have had a busy day at work.

Jane poured herself yet another brandy and Babycham with ice, a drink she'd enjoyed as a young woman in the carefree days of the early sixties. Back then, though, she had drunk from very different vessels. She held the glass up to the light and twisted it left to right, inspecting the contents while contemplating. The light lavished the heavy, exquisitely cut crystal, making it look as though she was holding a glass full of diamonds. No other glassware could have had the same effects, she thought. She would have preferred the plain champagne bowls of her youth, but there were no such common glasses in the cabinet.

She knew she was behaving like a typical frustrated housewife, stuck at home with no babies to rear, but there was no life for her now, either with or – worse – without Hugo. She felt overwhelmed by loneliness. She crossed the room to the stereo and put on an LP of her favourite composer, but even the most light-hearted of Vivaldi's pieces couldn't lift her mood. She stood in the window looking at the immaculate garden, tended by a professional gardener at Hugo's insistence even though she had wanted to take care of it herself, as she had their much smaller plot in London before they'd moved here. ('We need to keep up to the development's standards,

Jane. That's not a job for an amateur.')

Yes, the cottage garden she'd created in the capital's suburbs had had its occasional failed plantings and bare patches, but it was a happy place, echoing with their boys' laughter long after they had grown. In the landscaped perfection she was looking at now, nothing even looked like dying . . . except her marriage.

'To hell with it,' she said, this time switching to Bacardi and Coke. The alcohol was already starting to take hold of her, but she couldn't care less. She caught sight of herself in the mirror on the wall behind the bar. Her complexion was so reddened by the drinking, she looked almost sunburned under her honey-blonde shoulder-length bob.

She decided to write to an old friend in Warwick, recollecting the fun they used to have in the days before she married Hugo. As she struggled to gather her thoughts, the phone rang. Jane checked the time – it was precisely nine o'clock.

It was Celia. 'Jane, darling, I was wondering if you would like to come to the theatre tomorrow night?'

'Celia, that would be terrific,' Jane said, trying to keep her voice from slurring.

'How does *Romeo and Juliet* sound?' Celia asked.

Jane's smile evaporated at the very thought. The last thing she wanted was some love story to make her reflect on her relationship with Hugo, or lack of it. But Celia was a good friend, so it was worth going, if only to get out of the house.

'Lovely,' she replied. 'Is it formal?'

'Yes,' Celia replied, 'It's a premiere. Shakespeare with a twist. I've got an ankle-length dress and matching shawl by Jaeger. What about you?'

'Um, not sure,' Jane said, taking a sip of her drink, which wasn't sitting at all well with the brandy and Babycham.

'Look, Celia, honey, why don't you come over? Nobody wants to see me tonight! Come and join me for a nightcap.'

'You sound like you've had several nightcaps already,' said Celia, laughing. 'You should have called me earlier. I would have joined you. I'm in the middle of doing my hair now, darling, and then it will be time to get my beauty sleep.'

'I think I'll wear that two-piece I got at the boutique in the village,' said Jane, though even she could hear that her words now sounded like they'd been through a mincer.

'Get some sleep yourself, Jane,' said Celia. 'You sound like you need it. Drink some coffee first. I'll pick you up at seven o'clock tomorrow evening. The show starts at eight.' With that, she hung up.

Jane staggered awkwardly to the kitchen to follow Celia's advice. Her clumsy lack of coordination made her drop the coffee caddy from the shelf, the aromatic powder scattering across the floor. She bent to clean it up and hit her head on the edge of the worktop. Eventually settling for water, she drank three tumblers of it. Then she made her way up to bed, dreading the hangover she was expecting in the morning.

She sprawled across the bed in her nightgown and closed her eyes, but instantly the room became a whirling carousel. Her stomach heaved. She crawled to their en-suite bathroom and knelt with her head over the toilet bowl, awaiting the inevitable consequences of her indulgence. To her horror, she heard the front door slam as Hugo arrived home.

'Jane!' he called out. She heard him say 'What on earth . . .'

and realised he must have gone to the coffee-spattered kitchen. Then she heard footsteps on the stairs and looked up, mortified to find him watching her from the doorway as she clutched her white satin gown closed with one hand the second before she threw up.

'Something I ate,' she said, before retching again.

'Jane, how stupid do you think I am? I haven't seen you looking this rough in years. How much have you had to drink?' he asked, his voice calm but, she was gratified to hear, tinged with concern.

'Just a few. How about you? Did you have a nice "operation"?'

'Nice? What do you mean, "nice"?' he asked. 'It's my job. I work for us, not for fun.'

'That's what I used to think too,' she said. 'But now what I'm asking myself is, just how stupid do you think *I* am?'

12

Tuesday morning was as busy as usual. The first patient arrived in the recovery room at nine o'clock. 'OK, girls,' Claire said, 'let's rock and roll.'

Claire was feeling rather good, believing she had a lot to look forward to, however complicated. With her head full of Hugo, and not so much Richie, someone was bound to get hurt, but that was just the way of things.

Rhonda the Redhead checked in the next patient. Rhonda was a kind-hearted if slow-witted girl, a little sensitive, but reliable, with a laid-back persona that defied the fiery red-haired stereotype.

The rest of Claire's team went about their daily tasks with their usual calm efficiency, maintaining regular checks on the equipment used to aid the patients' recovery from anaesthetisation. At the busiest times, they could sometimes be wheeled in less than five minutes apart, and Claire reflected how lucky she was to have someone as calm and well organised as Libby as her number two. Thanks to her, things tended to run like clockwork. Claire sniffed the air. The whole department always had a clean, clinical scent about it, at least until Rebecca Maine began her mother-hen routine. Then it would smell more like a coffee shop.

She could detect no caffeine this morning, though, because there was no Rebecca Maine. She had taken a day off to visit a sick relative in Birmingham. To her disappointment, however, Hugo would not be in theatre today either. No major operations were scheduled, and Tim Dawson was more than competent to take care of the rest of his list. She clung to the hope that he would drop in anyway.

During her morning break Claire drifted over to chat with Jinny, who was busy demolishing a packet of rich tea biscuits with her coffee and leafing through the latest *Cosmo*. Claire smiled, gently patting Jinny's tummy. 'Just think, Jinny, I'm going to be a godmother. Who'd have thought it?' she said.

Jinny looked round the empty office in alarm. 'Shh, Claire. No telling, remember? At least not yet.'

'OK, OK, calm down. There's no one to hear. Anyway, I'm

just excited for you,' Claire stage-whispered, her eyes bulging in defence.

A voice came from the corridor outside and Claire's heart skipped a beat, because she was sure it had been Hugo's. With no time to undo the top button of her uniform, she just stood and pushed out her chest as Hugo entered Jinny's open-plan office en route to the medical room. 'Hello, ladies. How are we this fine morning?' The words were addressed to them both, but his eyes didn't leave Claire's as he spoke them. Then he was gone, leaving only the scent of his aftershave as lingering evidence of his presence.

Jinny screwed her face up, confused. 'Why is he here?' she asked. 'I thought he was off today.'

Claire shrugged her shoulders. 'Who cares? Just be grateful for small mercies, I say.'

'Oh, Claire,' Jinny frowned.

'Don't start with the lecture, Jin,' Claire said, only half joking.

As she returned to the recovery room, Claire tried to understand why even the mere sight of Hugo turned her into a quivering wreck. Yes, she fancied him like mad, but that was hardly a rarity. Claire hadn't been short of suitors during her time at Harvington and hadn't hesitated to invite into her bed any of them who took her fancy. This was the 1980s, after all, she reasoned. What was the point of being born beautiful if you weren't going to take advantage of it? At six months, her relationship with Richie was one of her longer pairings – many failed to make it past the first night – but despite his attentiveness and his success, not to mention her unexpected fidelity to him, she knew in her heart that he was really only a placeholder until what her mother would call 'Mr Right' came along. Until now, she had doubted that such a character existed. Hugo, though, provoked in her a whole new level of emotion, one that she had never before experienced. There was no other word for it but love.

'Are you all right, Claire?' asked Rhonda.

'Who, me? I'm fine,' she replied, picking up a clipboard and avoiding eye contact. 'Can you ring Wren Ward to see if they're ready for your patient, please?'

Libby gave her boss an old-fashioned look as Rhonda

ambled off.

'What?' said Claire.

'Anything you want to tell me?' asked Libby.

'Actually, yes, but not here and not now. Let's have a lunch in the canteen for a change, shall we? We can chat there, woman to woman.'

The morning passed uneventfully and at 1 p.m. the pair made their way to the staff canteen. With laden trays, they found a free table, out of earshot of anyone Claire knew. As they sat down, Libby flicked her hair back, distributing plates and cutlery from tray to table before blowing out a puff of air.

'Well?' she said.

Claire was silent. Her enthusiasm for sharing had suddenly evaporated.

'This is to do with Hugo Bowman, isn't it?' said Libby. 'I saw him walking through the department earlier, and then you came in looking like a schoolgirl who's got a crush on her teacher,' she added, confirming Claire's suspicion that she was one of the more observant members of Harvey General's staff as well as one of the most efficient.

'Well, since you've obviously worked it out for yourself, there's not much point denying it. I really don't know why, but I fancy him rotten. Talk about sex on legs! I bet that surprised you.'

Libby broke into laughter. 'Not really. In fact, I think it was plain for all to witness that something was up with you. If only you could have seen yourself – your face was a picture. I could feel the heat radiating from you as soon as you walked into the recovery room.'

'Oh no, please tell me you're kidding!' Claire said with a grimace, holding her hands together below her chin.

'I am not kidding. I don't know how you get away with it.'

'With what?' asked Claire innocently.

'Have you ever heard that saying "I can resist anything except temptation"? That describes you to a T.'

'Well, you're only young once,' Claire replied.

'OK, OK, don't rub it in,' said Libby, smiling.

'I didn't mean it like that, Libby. You're not old,' said Claire. 'What are you, fifty?'

'Forty-three, thanks very much, and old enough to know

better. Unlike you, apparently.'

'Oh dear, I've put my foot in it again, haven't I?' said Claire. 'Sorr-eee.'

'Fluttering your eyelashes won't work with me, Claire. Save it for your next conquest. Were you expecting me to wish you luck? "Woman to woman" you said? Well, it's about time you grew up. Trust me, going after a married consultant isn't going to end well.'

Not for the first time Claire was left wondering who was the senior staff member here. Despite out-ranking her, Claire on occasion felt a little inferior to the older woman, who had earned the respect shown to her by the team and had an air of authority about her. That was something Claire hadn't quite managed to achieve, which was a constant source of irritation. She also knew, though would never admit to anyone, that Libby was the glue holding the department together. If Libby left the job for any reason, she herself would have to either leave or step down for self-preservation. For now, though, she was happy to take the title and the money to match.

And if she could snare Hugo Bowman, she would no

longer need either.

***

As they left the canteen, Claire spotted Jane Bowman in the distance, heading down the corridor towards them. 'You go on, Libby,' she said. 'I meant to get myself a packet of crisps for later. I'll be along in a minute.'

She turned and allowed Jane to catch up with her.

'Claire, hi!'

'Oh, hi, Jane!' she said. 'How are you?'

'Oh, you know, getting by. Yourself?'

'Not bad. It seems like ages since we had a good old chinwag. You look great, by the way,' said Claire, noting the bags under Jane's eyes and the too-thick make-up applied in an attempt to create an artificially healthy complexion. Here was a woman with problems on her mind, but of what nature? 'You here for lunch?'

'Just getting a roll to take back to the office. Need to work through my break today. So much backlog with the records,' replied Jane.

Perhaps that was the problem, then.

'Poor you,' said Claire, surprised to find that she actually meant it. Jane really was a nice woman.

'Well, it's got to be done, hasn't it?'

'Mm, all work and no play, eh?'

'Not exactly, as it happens. I'm off to the theatre tonight to see some Shakespeare.'

'Oh!' said Claire. That was unexpected. She'd rather thought that if Hugo was playing away with Rebecca Maine, he and Jane would have long passed the going-out-together stage.

'Yes, with an old friend of mine,' Jane added.

Claire breathed a sigh of relief as she re-entered the brightly lit canteen. 'Very cultured. Which play are you seeing?'

'*Romeo and Juliet*,' said Jane.

'The original boy meets girl,' said Claire with a chuckle, but her laughter quickly evaporated as she saw a tear roll down Jane's face when she reached to retrieve a roll from the cabinet. Claire felt a tinge of guilt, but soon assuaged it with the rationalisation that she would, in fact, be doing Jane a good turn by ending her marriage. It was clearly already on its last legs, so a fresh start would do them all good. She chose a packet of crisps at random and they both paid at the till.

'Well, look, you have a good time tonight. Let's catch up soon, shall we?' said Claire.

'Oh, I will do. At least I'll be getting out,' said Jane. 'And, yes, let's talk soon. I really need a friend right now.'

On her way back to the department Claire passed a group of junior doctors and was gratified when all their eyes followed her progress, the men's with lust, the women's with distaste. 'Still got it, kiddo,' she said under her breath.

She heard a wolf whistle from behind. That was unusual; medics were usually more reserved. Unless . . .

She turned to see Len McClure standing with a big grin on his raddled face. With him was Hugo's registrar, Tim Dawson. He was wearing his white coat over his casual clothing: grey trousers and a teal jumper, which seem to complement his dark hair and pale skin.

'Please excuse my uncouth assistant,' said Tim. 'I'm training him up for a friend.'

'Hello, Tim,' said Claire. 'You kept us busy this morning.

Are you finished for the day?'

'No such luck. Got a meeting at two thirty,' he replied. 'It's a gathering of all the orthopods.'

'Oh, I see,' said Claire. 'I was wondering why your boss was here earlier.'

'Probably wanted to make sure I didn't saw the wrong leg off,' said Tim with a grin.

Claire's stomach turned at the thought. Once she was married to Hugo, she supposed she'd have to get used to such surgical black humour.

'Anyway, Claire, if you're at all interested, it's my birthday today, and tonight Hugo will be buying me a drink or few at the Liquor Clinic. You'd be welcome to join us.'

'Is that an open invite?' asked Len.

'To the recovery-room staff, yes,' said Tim. 'I shouldn't think you'll need one, Len. The bar's your second home, isn't it?'

Claire was grateful that Len had provided a distraction, for Tim's invitation had set her mind whirling too quickly to form a reply.

Tim returned his attention to her. 'Anyway, do feel free to pop in, won't you?'

'You know what theatre staff are like, Tim,' said Len. 'They never miss a do in the club.'

'Great! See you all later then.' He looked at his watch. 'Gotta go.'

Len accompanied Claire back to Theatres, talking the whole while, but Claire didn't register a word. The sole thought in her mind was: *Jane on a night out, Hugo at the social club and Rebecca out of town.* She could barely contain herself at the prospect that tonight would be the night she got Hugo on his own. She felt quite confident about seducing him. The one concern was Richie. He mustn't find out. Hugo was the target, but she still needed a Plan B, and Richie was it.

13

At seven thirty that night, Claire and Jinny arrived at the club without their partners, Claire having convinced Jinny that tonight's function was for hospital staff only. Richie had taken some persuading, but in the end had agreed to an extra practice session at the gun club instead, though he had insisted on being at Claire's flat before she arrived home, 'in case of burglars'. That ruled out the possibility of she and Hugo sharing her bed, but she decided Richie would be suspicious if she protested too much. Of course, she had no intention of sharing it with Richie either, but she'd worry about that later. With a bit of luck, before long it wouldn't matter how suspicious he was.

The late shift had just finished and, as the club began to fill with staff, the atmosphere was starting to liven up. Claire and Jinny had just reached the bar when Hugo and Tim arrived.

'I'll go first,' said Jinny. 'Two slimline tonics with ice and lemon, please, Steve, since it's a work night.' Claire gave Jinny a blank look. 'Actually, make that second one a large red wine,' she added.

'That's one pound forty to you,' said Steve, nodding a hello at Hugo as Jinny fumbled with her purse.

Hugo brought out his wallet. 'That's fine, I'll pay for these. And two pints of best, please, Steve.'

Hugo's and Claire's eyes met again as she thanked him with a smile. 'Happy birthday, Tim,' she said, raising her glass. 'There's a table over there, Jinny.' She looked up at Hugo. 'It's big enough for four.'

The two women went to sit down. A band was setting up at the other end of the club, young musicians wandering in and out with various pieces of equipment. A few minutes later Hugo and Tim casually left the bar and headed towards Claire and Jinny, who nudged each other like a pair of excited schoolgirls. Claire, shaking with nerves at the prospect of finally achieving her goal, rummaged in her handbag for her cigarettes and lighter, thinking it would calm her to have a smoke. The men stopped midway across the room, deep in conversation, provoking even more anxiety in Claire, before eventually arriving at the table and sitting down to join them.

Noticing that Claire seemed dumbstruck, Jinny broke the ice: 'It's very brave of you, Tim, arranging a birthday drink in the social club. It can get a bit rowdy in here.'

'Why not?' Hugo replied for him. His eyes switched from Jinny's to Claire's as he raised his glass. 'Most of us like to party.'

Claire was uncharacteristically flustered, wishing the wine would take effect more quickly. She took a deep pull her cigarette before stubbing it out. 'Anyone for another?' she asked knocking back the last drop in her glass.

Tim looked a little uncomfortable as he offered to get the next round, apparently surprised by the chemistry between Hugo and Claire.

'So, how was your meeting today, Hugo?' Claire asked as Tim made for the bar.

'My meeting? Oh – the meeting. Fine.'

Claire was relieved to see that Hugo seemed just as distracted by her as she was by him.

Tim returned with the drinks and Steve increased the volume of the jukebox to match the crowd noise in the room.

The conversation flowed more easily with the drinks, and the quartet had to lean in ever closer to hear each other. Then a sudden crash of cymbals from the stage was followed by a short speech of introduction by the band's front man before they went straight into their first song – a Rolling Stones cover – with all the energy of the real thing.

To Claire's delight, Hugo was a lot friendlier and more down to earth than she had expected, he and Tim taking it in turns to deliver amusing anecdotes and the odd joke. In the end, it seemed they were in good-natured competition for the title of funniest man in the room.

By now, most of the theatre department staff had arrived – including Len, with his big personality. 'Ay, up, everybody, I'll 'ave you all dancing on the tables by the end of the night,' he announced as he boogied through the room to the bar. There was a raucous laugh, and everyone cheered him along.

Iain, his Glaswegian assistant, was first up, swaying his hips with his pint above his head. 'That's it, lad!' cried Len. 'See how he's following in my footsteps?'

By eleven, the bar was calling for last orders and the crowd were calling for an encore from the band, who had displayed an impressive show of talent. Steve collected empty glasses from the tables, asking the owners of the rest to drink up and leave as he went and avoiding eye contact, something he usually did when he wished to be taken seriously. Once the crowd had been reduced to just the regulars, the curtains were pulled shut for a lock-in. On went the jukebox again, though now quite low, and the drinking continued, with Len being the centre of attention as usual.

Hugo and Tim were engaged in a conversation about the return of Hong Kong to China in 1997, which Claire couldn't care less about, so she and Jinny took the opportunity to disappear to the ladies' toilets.

'Claire, what time are you staying until?' asked Jinny.

'I'm not sure. I'm quite enjoying the company, to be honest,' said Claire, deciding against telling Jinny that, ideally, her and Hugo's night wouldn't be ending for several hours yet.

'The boys will be expecting us, though.'

'I know. Look, if you need to get back to your Brian, just go on. I can order a cab when I'm ready.'

'I don't like the idea of leaving you on your own, Claire.'

'I won't be on my own. I'm with two of the country's top orthopaedic surgeons. What do you think they're going to do – drug me and fit a new hip while I'm unconscious? Honestly, I'll be fine. Just stay another half hour, then go.'

They returned to their table, where the men were now discussing the miners' strike. As Claire sat down, the stool wobbled slightly, causing her to blush and giggle.

Hugo looked up, raising his eyebrows in amusement. Tim laughed.

'Perhaps we should call it a night,' said Hugo.

Jinny looked at her watch. 'Crumbs, it's 12.30 a.m.! My other half will be wondering where I've got to. Thank you for a lovely evening, Tim, Mr Bowman, but I really must go now.' She looked at Claire and angled her head towards the door. 'Coming?'

'No. Seriously, Jinny, you go on.'

Tim stood up, swaying slightly. 'Well, I could do with some beauty sleep myself. Shall we share a cab, Jinny? There'll be one on the rank near the hospital. I'll have a look.'

'My car's outside, Tim. I'll give you a lift.'

'Perfect. I'll see you out there,' said Tim.

After giving Claire a brief hug, Jinny followed him out.

'That just leaves you and me, then, Claire. Would you like another drink, or might I offer you a lift too? As Jinny said, it is a work night, after all. I've only had a couple of shandies, so you'll be quite safe.'

It looked like Plan A might be working. 'Thanks, that would be great, so long as you don't mind,' she said.

'Not at all. In fact, it would be a pleasure.'

They chatted about work throughout the short journey to Well Street, Claire feeling regal inside Hugo's top-of-the-range Mercedes, which was even more luxurious than Richie's new Volvo. As they turned into her road, it occurred to her that Richie might be watching from the window of the flat for her to return.

'Just here will do,' she said. The people at the end of the road were having some work done and a skip had been left outside their house. She directed Hugo to pull in behind it, where they'd be hidden from prying eyes. The engine was still running when she leaned over to give Hugo an alcohol-emboldened kiss on the cheek.

He leaned back and looked at her approvingly. 'You are one beautiful woman, do you know that?' he asked her.

This was it! He was nibbling at the bait. She mustn't let him get away now. She had to play this one just right.

'We're all beautiful after a couple of pints,' she said, deciding that false modesty would reel him in more reliably than brazenness.

'But I don't usually date women with boyfriends.'

Claire's heart sank, but her expression remained unchanged, though her mind was racing. What she said next could define her future.

'And I don't usually date married men,' she said, without unlocking her gaze from his. 'But . . .'

' . . . there are exceptions to every rule,' he finished the sentence for her and switched off the engine.

Slowly, inexorably, they drew ever closer until their lips made contact, almost chastely at first, and then harder. It was as though that first touch confirmed a mutual feeling of intensity between them, dismissing any inhibitions.

Suddenly they were kissing passionately, lost in the moment and relishing every second. Claire immersed herself in his strong, clean aura and the warm comfort of his powerful arms as he held her to him.

'God, you smell good,' said Hugo, provoking a millisecond of guilt as she recalled that the expensive perfume she was wearing had been a surprise present from Richie.

The passion consumed them for a while, until they broke apart for air. Still her mind was working. Hugo was firmly hooked now, but there was still work to be done before he was safely in the net. Perhaps it was a good thing that Richie was in the flat. The smart move now was to leave Hugo wanting more, but she doubted she could have trusted herself not to go further if she'd had a choice. She tidied herself before leaving the car, pouting her lips as she did so.

'Thanks for the lift,' she said, opening the car door. 'It was lovely.'

She stood and watched as he drove off, his eyes still on her through his door mirror.

When she reached her flat, she put the key in the lock and turned it slowly, trying not to make a sound. She then slipped off her shoes in the hallway and tiptoed upstairs. In the bathroom she threw her hair back, splashed her face with hot water and then made a half-hearted attempt at removing her make-up with one hand while holding on to the sink with the other to steady herself. She squinted at her hazy reflection in the steamed-up mirror, then jumped when she saw a figure standing behind her. 'Richie?' she said softly, but when she turned her head there was no one there. She crossed to the doorway and peered out, looking and listening with her heart pounding.

'Ritch, is that you?' she whispered into the darkness.

There was no reply. He must have got bored of waiting and gone home. Too tired and woozy to think about it, she tiptoed to her bed and quickly passed into a deep sleep. She woke again after two hours, her head pounding but feeling too wrecked even to fetch a tablet. Before she fell asleep again, she could have sworn she saw Richie staring at her from the bedroom door.

14

The recovery room's emergency buzzer was sounding as, for the first time in Claire's experience, two people in her care were suffering a cardiac arrest simultaneously. This couldn't have happened at a worse time. Claire was on her own in the recovery room, all the other staff having left either for lunch or a meeting. She looked helplessly at the lights flashing over the two stricken patients' beds, which were, oddly enough, adjacent to each other. Len ran in with the crash cart and positioned it in the space between them.

'Here you are, Sister. Time to earn your salary,' he said.

'But what do I do, Len?' said Claire. 'I've got two emergencies and only one defibrillator. Can you do CPR?'

'Not in my job description, love. I'm just the ODA. This is your responsibility. You'll just have to decide which one you want to save more. I've got a coin you can toss, if that helps. Anyway, got to go; there's a pint with my name on it.'

Claire ran across to the cart. All she could do was assess the patients' conditions and then make a decision. She registered that the beds were occupied by a man and a woman but that was all. The buzzer vibrated through her skull, preventing her from thinking straight. She grabbed one arm of each patient feeling for a pulse. Both were weak and thready. She lifted the pads of the defibrillator, knowing that she was literally holding two people's lives in her hands. What to do? And still the buzzer sounded.

'For God's sake, will someone turn off that bloody noise!' she shouted.

Claire gasped for air as she pushed away the quilt cover and woke to the insistent sound of her alarm clock. Sighing with relief, she thumped the snooze button and lay still for five minutes to collect her thoughts. 'Oh God, my head!' she moaned.

She crawled out of bed, feeling delicate as bone china, and headed downstairs, piling her hair on top of her head. A glass of water tasted awful, but a mug of filtered coffee did a lot to revive her. The last thing she felt like today was going to work, and not just because of her hangover; she could cope with that, but the thought of Hugo seeing her in this condition filled her with dread. She decided it would be wise to ring Libby right now. She had a reliable character; maybe she could help.

Claire found Libby's home number in the little floral address book next to the phone and dialled. On the sixth ring someone answered, but as Claire began to speak she realised she was listening to Libby's answerphone message. Claire looked at her watch – she was already an hour late for work – and rang the unit. Paula picked up and transferred her to Jinny.

'What time did you roll in last night, you dirty stop-out? And how did it go with you know who?' said Jinny.

'Not now, Jinny,' Claire told her. 'Listen, do me a favour. I can't get in until midday and I need someone to cover.'

'In other words, you're hung over,' replied Jinny. 'Don't worry. Libby is already in the unit. I'll tell her you've had some sort of emergency while you fire up the Alka-Seltzer.'

'You're a star. I did try to ring Libby earlier, actually; I was wondering why she wasn't at home. OK, well, I'll see you later, and remember – mum's the word.'

'For us both,' laughed Jinny. They hung up.

Claire walked back to the kitchen, still feeling fragile, and refilled her mug with coffee. She was a lot more relaxed now that things were under control, and a bacon sandwich for breakfast was starting to seem like a good idea. As she opened the fridge door, she spotted a scribbled note on the worktop: *Hope you got up OK. I dozed off on the sofa. Had to leave early but I set your alarm first in case you were sparko. See you later, Richie x.*

So he *had* been in the flat last night. She thought how considerate he was, but she was also perturbed by the fact that his side of the bed hadn't been used. That wasn't like him. Had he spotted her and Hugo kissing? Perhaps the skip hadn't been tall enough to hide them from view. Had the interior light been on in the car, making them easy to see? She couldn't remember; she had been too preoccupied with Hugo to care. She walked to the spare room and found a mug half full of tea and the bedding ruffled. She returned to the living room and stood staring at the sofa as though it could provide her with an answer, thinking and biting her bottom lip. The phone rang, making her jump. She lifted the receiver, fully expecting to hear

Libby's voice informing her of problems at work – her conscience pricking her.

'Hello?'

There was a pause, and then, 'You made it out of bed, I see.'

Richie.

'Oh, it's you! God, I feel rough,' she told him.

'I'm not surprised, the state you were in last night.'

'Ugh! I can't do that again,' she replied.

'We'll have a quiet night in tonight, then. You haven't forgotten I'm coming over, have you? You promised to cook dinner, remember?'

She grimaced, recalling the trade-off she'd had to make for going out without him last night, but said nothing.

'I might be late, though,' he said. 'Got a sales meeting after work. They can drag on a bit. I'll be there by eight at the latest, though.'

'That's OK,' said Claire, thinking she wouldn't mind too much if it lasted all night.

'Throwing a sickie today, I take it?' he added.

'Certainly not! I'm doing a late shift today,' which was factually accurate, if not entirely honest. 'Richie, can I ask you something?'

'Anything – apart from my PIN number,' he said with a laugh.

'No, I'm serious. This might seem a bit odd but, were you looking at me in the bathroom last night when I came in? Or from the bedroom door? I tried to talk to you, but you didn't answer.'

'What do you think I am, Claire? Some kind of peeping Tom?' He sounded offended. 'I didn't even hear you come in. I looked in on you during the night to make sure you were still breathing, but that's all. I could tell you'd had a skinful from the way your make-up was smeared all over your face. You never let yourself look such a mess except when you're drunk.'

'But I thought I saw –'

'Whatever you thought you saw was in your head, Claire.'

15

Jane, too, woke in a bed that was occupied on her side only. In her case, though, the reason was vacation rather than absence. As she went downstairs to fill the kettle she could hear her husband puffing and panting in their gym, which was situated next to the kitchen and accessible via an internal door. It had originally comprised half of the property's four-car garage, but Hugo had wanted it converted.

Jane almost floated into the lounge, wearing a white satin dressing gown over a matching nightie. She pulled back the curtains in a not-so-angelic fashion and returned to the kitchen to make her cup of tea. Hugo eventually came in from the gym, sweating profusely, and as he propped himself against the breakfast bar, a little breathless, said, 'That's better.'

Jane stood holding her tea with her back to the kitchen sink, haloed by the sun streaming in from the window behind, and took a long sip as she stared at him. *How ridiculous*, she thought. *Who's he trying to impress?* Jane resented the fact that, in over twenty years of marriage and despite her long-held suspicions, she had yet to find a shred of incontrovertible evidence that Hugo had ever had an affair. Or affairs. He had long been a flirt, but had always shrugged that off as his way of keeping his nursing staff happy and engaged. How far he would actually take such behaviour remained to be seen – by her, at least.

Despite the fact that she was only three years shy of fifty, Jane sometimes felt very naive in the ways of the world. She wished she was a bit more streetwise, like Claire Frazer. Now there was someone who could have men eating out of her hand. She certainly wouldn't let one walk all over her. Part of the reason she had courted the younger woman's friendship was in the hope that she could find out whether Hugo was carrying on with anyone at the hospital. If anyone would know, it would be Claire. Perhaps some of her new friend's chutzpah would rub off on her.

'No sugar for me, remember,' he said. 'I'm cutting down.'

She automatically turned to pour him a cup of tea and was immediately irritated. 'Morning, Jane, how was the theatre last night? What did you see? Glad you enjoyed yourself, darling!' she ranted sarcastically. 'Maybe we could go to dinner this week and have a nice talk about why our marriage is *so fucking boring*,' she continued, slamming the mug of tea down on the worktop. She stood and studied his face for a moment as the spilled tea puddled and began to drip over the edge and onto the floor.

Hugo took a gulp from the now half-empty mug and said, 'Sorry, Jane, I can't handle one of your tantrums now. I'm going to watch the news.'

'Neither can I!' she called after him as he left the kitchen. 'It's pathetic. In fact, the whole thing is pathetic. *You're* pathetic. Out with some fancy woman half the night. Half your age too, I expect.' With that, she stormed upstairs to get dressed and go shopping. What she really wished she could buy, though, was some of his attention.

Rather than switching on the TV, Hugo followed her, calling from the foot of the stairs, 'Look, Jane, I'm a consultant with a standing to maintain, and I have to mix with staff and colleagues, sometimes even socially. It goes with the territory.'

Jane, who was almost at the top of the staircase, swung round to face him. 'Well, it all depends on what you mean by "social". I know you're up to more than just socialising for appearances' sake.'

'That's absurd,' he replied. 'What do you mean by that? Last night it was Tim's birthday. We had a few drinks, that's all. You could have come yourself, if you hadn't been swanning off to the theatre with Celia.' He advanced up the stairs towards her and reached the third step from the top with a face like thunder. 'To be honest, Jane, I've just about had enough of you and your accusations.'

Jane was raging inside. 'I'll push you down these bloody stairs if you come any closer,' she threatened. 'I mean it!'

Hugo stopped in his tracks.

'That surprised you, didn't it? In fact, you're looking a bit scared now. Well, Mister Big-Shot Consultant, you're not the only one in this house who's had enough. Just go and impress your little nurses at work and leave me alone!'

She went to the bedroom and stripped off to have a shower. As she pulled her hair back, she regretted her threat of violence, but he had enraged her. Why, just for once, couldn't he make the time to give her a little of the attention she'd once craved? In fact, still craved, because deep down she had never stopped loving him. He, on the other hand, seemed to have forgotten she existed.

She had been coping with his secrecy, his strange behaviour and his lack of interest in their relationship for some time. They were a couple who had everything – wealth, standing, a beautiful home. How had their marriage ended up in such desperate straits? Whatever the reason, he was clearly confused and dissatisfied while she was feeling ever more lonely and neglected. Trying to clutch at the remains of the marriage and keep her sanity was proving to be quite a task, perhaps an impossible one.

For years she had tried to keep the seriousness of the situation from their two sons, but even they were aware that something was wrong, though not of the full extent. In fact, she and Hugo behaved so well in public that nobody would have suspected anything at all.

As she emerged from the shower ten minutes later she

heard the sound of golf clubs rattling. 'I've got a four-ball booked,' he called out, 'and I'll probably have lunch up there today.'

Jane wrapped herself in a bathrobe and walked to the window to watch him go.

Jeff Glass had returned as promised to clean the windows and was leaning his ladder against the front of the house as Hugo left.

'Morning, Mr Bowman. Off to improve your handicap, are you?'

'On the contrary, young man, I'm leaving it behind,' Hugo replied, leaving Jeff with a puzzled look on his face as he drove off at speed. Jeff glanced up and saw Jane at the window. 'Morning, Mrs B,' he called, giving a wave. 'I'll start round the back, shall I?'

Jane went down to the kitchen and opened the back door as Jeff came round the corner of the house. 'Hi, Jeff. I'd forgotten all about you coming today. How are you feeling now?'

'Much better, thanks, Mrs B. How about you? You look a

bit glum, if you don't mind me saying.'

'Really, I'm fine.' She sighed. 'Thanks for asking, though. Coffee?'

'Let me do the back first, and then I'll have a break,' he said.

As Jane watched him climb the ladder, she thought about how gentlemanly he was, and how good looking. She pottered round the kitchen as he worked, cleaning up the tea she'd spilled earlier, and had just poured the coffees when he came in.

'Penny for your thoughts,' he said, as she stared into her cup vacantly.

She glanced wearily up at him.

'Do you want to talk about it?' he asked.

She smiled. 'There's not a lot to say, really.'

'I'm a good listener,' he replied.

She looked at him warmly. 'No, I'm all right, Jeff, honestly. What about you?' she asked him, flicking her blonde hair to the side.

'Me?'

'Mm, how are things with you?' she pressed.

'Well . . . not good, if I'm honest,' he said. 'I found out at the weekend that Sharon, that's my wife, has been seeing someone else. We had a big bust-up on Saturday, and she told me on Sunday that they were going to set up home together.'

What a waste, thought Jane. 'Oh, you poor thing!' she said. 'Sit down and tell me about it. If you want to, that is. I'm a good listener too,' she added. 'It's so sad when a relationship breaks down.' *And I should know*, she reflected ruefully.

'Thanks. That's why I wasn't myself on Monday. I'm afraid I was doing the poor old Chinese takeaway a disservice.'

'Do you have any children?'

'No, thank goodness. We tried, but it never happened. Just as well, really. Even now, I'm still wondering where it all went wrong, because as far as I thought, everything was fine with both of us. I really didn't have a clue.' He stared into space for a moment, then shook his head and stood, hitching up his trousers. 'You look after yourself, Mrs B. You look like you've lost your sparkle lately too. You know where I am if ever you need a chat,' he added. 'Right, then, better get on with it.

Those front windows won't clean themselves.'

Jane sat thinking for a moment after Jeff left. Was her unhappiness really that obvious? It was coming to something when your window cleaner was more attuned to your mood than your husband.

At that point, the phone rang. It was Celia. 'Jane, darling! What are you doing this afternoon?'

'I was planning on painting,' Jane replied.

'Oh, give it a miss and have lunch with me instead. I have some news.'

Jane rolled her eyes. She'd probably just bought a new scarf. Everything was a mystery with Celia. 'What time?'

'Two thirty?'

'OK, I'll be there,' Jane agreed, and replaced the receiver.

What Jeff had said earlier had unsettled her. She was a sensitive person and private about her personal life, disclosing her problems only when they became too much to bear, but Jeff's offer of a sympathetic ear was tempting. In fact, the prospect of spending any time at all with him was very appealing.

'Admit it, Jane, you fancy him,' she said to herself. It was not like he was a stranger, after all; he had been their window cleaner ever since they'd moved in. She thought he found her attractive too, although since both were married, neither of them would have seriously entertained the thought of acting on it. Now, though, he was free. And as for her, well, the more she thought about Hugo and his antics, the more she felt she could rationalise her own behaviour. Suppose she was wrong though, and just made a fool of herself trying to attract a younger man? Then she had a lightbulb moment: *What would Claire Frazer do?*

With that thought in her head, the rest was easy. She almost ran up the stairs, anxious not to miss her opportunity to put her plan into practice. From the landing, she could hear Jeff's ladder being moved to the master bedroom window and his footsteps ascending the rungs. When they stopped, she went into action, walking casually into the room, discarding her robe and crossing to the wardrobe stark naked, her head down as though engrossed in thought and taking care to avoid looking in his direction. Though she said it herself, her body was still firm and curvaceous, and she hoped he was thinking the same thing.

Suddenly, there was a thump against the window. She looked round to see and Jeff disappearing to one side with the ladder following him.

Jane was panicking as she ran from the wardrobe to the window. What if she'd killed him? To her relief, Jeff was lying just a few feet below her, his fall luckily broken by the tall, thick hedge that surrounded the front garden. She grabbed the bathrobe and, gasping for breath, ran downstairs to the front door. With one hand over her mouth and the other clasping shut the untied robe, she stood in the doorway. Jeff clambered down from the hedge, groaning and stretching his back.

'My God, Jeff,' she said, reaching out to him, 'are you all right?'

Jeff looked up at Jane and, staring at her now wide-open bathrobe, suggested she go back inside. 'Quick, or we'll have the neighbours talking. This is worse than a *Carry On* film!'

At that point, they both became overwhelmed by the ridiculous nature of the situation and, laughing fit to burst, Jane clasped the robe shut, turned and went back into the house, leaving the front door open behind her. Jeff followed her in and gently pushed the door closed. Their laughter soon died as they stood in the hallway facing each other in anticipation. Jane let the robe fall open again. Jeff raised his hand and stroked her face softly and slowly before tenderly kissing her lips. For Jane, time seemed to stand still for a moment, and then rush to warp speed as they kissed passionately, their hearts pounding, as between them they frantically released his clothing. With one smooth movement, he lifted her onto the hall table and entered her, both of them drunk with passion.

Afterwards, they went up to the bedroom and made love once again, taking their time to pleasure each other. Jane had almost forgotten how wonderful sex could be.

'You know, I've always fancied you something rotten, Mrs B, but I never thought anything would ever come of it, what with us being so different and all.'

Jane smiled at the realisation that the fun and attention she craved from her husband Hugo but could never obtain had been literally arriving on her doorstep once a month.

The minutes ticked away. The bedside phone rang twice, but they paid it no mind.

Eventually, they dozed off, holding each other closely and waking only when the phone rang again. This time Jane answered it. It was Celia.

'Jane, where are you? It's three o'clock.'

But Jane had lost interest in the whole idea of meeting up. She apologised and rang off.

'I ought to get dressed,' she whispered, kissing him. 'And you ought to leave. Hugo could come back at any time.'

Jeff went down to the hall to find his clothes while Jane threw on some leggings and a jumper before joining him.

'You'd best use the kitchen door, Jeff.'

'I don't suppose we could . . .' he said.

'No, seriously, you have to go.'

'No problem, Mrs B. You're so beautiful, do you know that?' he said.

'I do now,' said Jane.

'Same time next month, then?'

'For the windows, yes. For the extras, we'll see,' said Jane.

A fling was all she'd wanted; anything more than that could end up being far too complicated. 'Here's your money,' she added, giving him the five-pound note she'd left out to pay him with. It felt like a strange transaction.

'Thanks for that,' said Jeff. 'And for . . . you know.'

'Well, thank you too,' she said, giving him a peck on the cheek. 'And Jeff?'

'Yes, Mrs B?'

'I think you'd better start calling me Jane, don't you?'

16

Claire hung up the phone, unsettled by her conversation with Richie. Had she really been seeing things in the night? Perhaps she should reduce her alcohol intake for a while. She returned to bed and dozed fitfully for a couple of hours. She woke at eleven thirty, less hung over but even more tired, before remembering that she had told Jinny she would be at the department for midday. She leapt from the bed and hurriedly applied her make-up before wriggling into her uniform.

'Bloody hell, Claire,' she chided herself, 'you can't even be late on time!'

She sped her way to the hospital and parked her Mini Cooper just as the hands on the dashboard clock ticked over to noon. She ran to the recovery room and pushed open the door.

'Sorry, the traffic was –'

Her words dried up as half a dozen heads turned to look at her. She was used to being looked at, but not like this. Every member of staff was wearing the same mournful expression.

'What? What is it?' said Claire.

Libby emerged from the small group of nurses and walked towards her. 'Claire, we've just heard. It's Karen Thomas,' she said.

Little mousy Karen, the second-year student who was scared of her own shadow? What could she possibly have done to upset everyone?

'We've just been told that she was found dead this morning,' Libby continued.

'Dead?' said Claire. 'How?'

'Suicide, I've heard,' said Libby. 'She lived in the nurses' quarters and the housekeeper found her in the bath with her wrists cut when she went in to clean her room.'

'God, that's horrible. But she was only in here on Monday. She was fine then,' said Claire. Then she thought back to the bitten-down fingernails she'd noticed, and the lack of eye contact. Had she really been fine? She hadn't been under Claire's supervision for over half a year, but she felt a twinge of guilt nevertheless.

Amanda Stoles, the first-year student, took a step forward.

'I could tell something wasn't right when I was speaking to her,' she said, confirming what Claire had been thinking.

'That's awful,' said Claire. 'I feel like I should have done something to help her.'

'It's not your fault, Claire,' said Libby. 'But it does go to show what a strain these girls are under. This is the second one in under a year. Remember Amy Carter last November?'

'Oh yes, that's right,' said Claire. 'That was an unusual one – a suicide with no note. Len's always maintained there was something mysterious about that. Still, you know what Len's like. Did Karen leave one?'

Libby frowned. 'A note? Yes, she did. Apparently it was because her lover had found someone else.'

'Really? I didn't even know she had a boyfriend,' said Claire.

'She didn't,' said Rhonda, 'but she had a girlfriend!' she added triumphantly.

'And what difference does that make?' said Claire sharply. For all her faults, Claire disliked bitchiness.

'Well, you know . . .' said Rhonda lamely.

'No, I don't know, and if you've nothing sympathetic to add, I'd suggest you get on with what you're being paid to do,' said Claire. Rhonda blushed scarlet and made a hasty exit.

Libby and Claire crossed to the admin desk.

'Well,' said Claire, 'I wasn't expecting that.'

'That she was a lesbian, you mean?' replied Libby. 'None of us were. Even the note she left didn't mention it – just the name Alex. Short for Alexandra, it turned out. The truth only came out because she'd put down this Alex as next of kin. It wasn't until the police got in touch with the news that anyone realised. Still, each to their own, I suppose.'

'Oh, I'm not going to judge her, Libby. It's just . . .'

'I know, Claire; we're not used to this, are we, really?' said Libby.

'It must have been awful for the housekeeper,' said Claire. Then a thought struck her. 'God! It wasn't the same one who found Amy Carter, was it?'

'No, thank goodness. Can you imagine it, though – opening the bathroom door and finding a body? All that blood! Even as a nurse I'd have trouble coping with that, let alone some poor woman employed to do the dusting.' Libby shuddered for a moment at the thought as she told Claire what she knew. 'Her parents are coming down from Norfolk to identify the body.'

The recovery room's busy schedule allowed little time for grief, and the staff were soon back in full swing as a steady flow of patients were wheeled in from theatre and back to the wards. No complications arose, and Claire was relieved that the list was running so well, reflecting that the past twenty-four hours had already provided more than enough shocks to her system for one day.

It was now half past four and the day shift was coming to an end. Libby began the usual end-of-day check that post-op supplies were restocked and drugs were reordered. Maria da Sousa recovered the last patient while Claire checked that the case notes were written up correctly. After two sets of good observations, the ward was called to ensure that they were ready to receive him.

As they prepared to leave, Claire and Libby talked about how they would spend their respective evenings.

'Feet up with a good book for me,' said Libby. 'How about you, Claire?'

'I'm not sure yet. Richie's coming round later tonight, so I'll probably get us a takeaway and a video. Nothing too strenuous,' she said with a chuckle. 'I could do with staying in, actually, just to have a break from the alcohol.'

'I should think so, burning the candle at both ends,' said Libby, smiling. 'Jinny said you had a toothache this morning, but I'm guessing it was more of a raging headache after Tim Dawson's birthday bash last night.'

They walked out of the hospital together and across to the car park to go their separate ways. Libby waved as she drove off towards the exit barrier. As Claire popped a cassette into the player she saw Hugo in her rear-view mirror and felt a slightly panicked frisson of excitement. He was standing outside the main entrance door, speaking to someone inside. She watched as he finished the conversation with whoever it was and began trembling with excitement as he walked over to her car. She wound down the window as he approached.

'And how are you today, Sister Frazer?' he asked her.

'Very well, Mr Bowman, thank you for asking. And your good self, sir?'

'All the better for seeing you,' he said with a smile.

Smooth talker, she thought, enjoying the flattery none the less.

'Seriously, I was wondering whether you might be free later,' he asked.

'Erm, I might be,' she said, trying to ignore the nagging feeling that she had something else to do.

'Good. In that case, perhaps we could meet,' he said. 'I feel as though we have unfinished business after last night.'

Then the nagging feeling resolved into the realisation that she had agreed to see Richie later as part of the deal she'd made to go out the night before. Her instinct was to put her boyfriend off, but if she stood him up again tonight, he was going to suspect something. She might have Hugo on her fishing line, but he wasn't landed yet. She couldn't risk losing her Plan B. 'I'd love to, but actually, I can't,' she said. 'I've just remembered, I've already planned something this evening.'

'That's a pity,' said Hugo. 'We'll have to make it another

time, then. I'm sure it will be worth the wait.'

Before Claire could reply, Hugo brushed her cheek gently with his fingers, turned on his heel and walked back towards the hospital, leaving her with a stomach full of butterflies that were only just closing their wings by the time she arrived home. She heeled the front door behind her, pocketed her keys, kicked off her shoes and made her way upstairs. In the lounge, she dropped her bag on the floor next to the sofa and slumped down on it, exhausted. The day's events whirled through her mind, the euphoria of her burgeoning affair with Hugo, the tragedy of Karen's death, the fear that Richie would abandon her if he discovered what she'd been up to. But, even though it was only six o'clock, her overwhelming feeling was one of tiredness, and this sofa really was so comfortable . . .

17

As Claire slept, Jinny and Brian were busy working their way through the hearty cottage pie she'd just cooked. Jinny still enjoyed her food in generous amounts, relishing the fact that she now had an excuse to put on a few extra pounds. The only downside she had experienced during the pregnancy was fatigue, especially at the end of a long shift, when she often felt jaded and even more glad than usual to be going home. She'd been dreading morning sickness ever since she'd found out she was pregnant, but so far, and to her great relief, it hadn't put in an appearance.

Brian was going away the following morning on a two-day training course and wouldn't be back until late on Friday. Jinny hated the thought of them spending even a single night apart, but she accepted that it was the price they must pay for success. Her husband was a parts-store manager at a large electrical wholesaler, and needed to stay abreast of the latest technology and regulations.

Over dinner, Brian talked about his day's work. Jinny liked to listen as he told her about the people who came to him in search of spare parts. Brian was a wonderful storyteller, and he described his customers in such detail that she almost felt she knew them all personally. He was passionate about his job, and it was a matter of pride to him that he was able to supply any item he was asked for. Tonight's discussion was about six-gang, two-way flush switch units, which sounded to her like a cross between a street fight and a supercharged toilet cistern, but she nodded in what she hoped was all the right places as she immersed herself in his gentle voice. She loved the fact that he was ambitious and keen to climb the social ladder, especially now they were having their first baby. She felt proud of him and utterly confident of their long-term future together.

After dinner, Brian took a cold Guinness from the fridge. He kissed Jinny's neck and held her closely for a moment before he opened the can. The phone rang; on the line was Jinny's mother, asking if it would be convenient for her and her husband to visit the following Sunday.

'Will that be OK, Brian?' whispered Jinny, her hand over

the mouthpiece.

'Of course,' said Brian. 'I love seeing your parents.'

He would take her father for a drink at the local while she cooked a roast lunch with her mother and caught up on gossip.

Jinny confirmed a time of eleven o'clock. 'And I've got some good news, Mum, so don't be late!'

After the dishes were done – Brian washed, Jinny wiped – they snuggled up in front of the TV, Brian stroking Jinny's hair while he sipped his beer.

As Jinny immersed herself in *Coronation Street*, Brian's eyes closed. Jinny turned down the volume and stared at his handsome face. She thought what a good father he was going to make, and how much she was enjoying her pregnancy, even though she felt so tired most of the time. He stirred and opened his eyes briefly, smiled, kissed her forehead and squeezed her tight before closing them again.

Jinny wondered who the baby would take after, his side or hers. She hoped it would be his, especially if it was a girl, so their daughter wouldn't have to watch her weight all the time. But, truth be told, it didn't matter so long as the baby was healthy. 'That's all people want in the end,' she said quietly. That and a happy marriage.

Brian woke slowly, giving her a loving smile. 'Cup of tea, sweetheart?' she asked.

'You stay there, I'll make it,' he said, getting up.

They watched TV for a while longer, then Brian looked at his watch. 'Ten o'clock, and time we were in bed, darling,' he said, helping her up from the sofa. In the bathroom he held her from behind as she rinsed her face and patted it dry. 'I love you so much, Virginia,' he said, kissing her neck tenderly. 'You're going to be a great mum.'

Looking at their reflection in the mirror set her tingling all over. They made such a handsome couple. She turned, intending to kiss him, but he took her hand and led her to the bed instead.

18

Jane recognised the familiar engine note of Hugo's Mercedes as it pulled into the drive just as the *News at Ten* was starting. She wondered where he'd spent the last four hours, then realised she no longer had the right to care. She heard his key turn in the lock and he breezed in jauntily. 'Hi,' he called out, removing his jacket. 'Late team meeting. Sorry.'

She believed that as much as she believed Margaret Thatcher would be inviting Arthur Scargill to Christmas dinner this year, but her afternoon with Jeff had undercut the moral high ground she usually felt justified in occupying, and she responded with a neutral 'Don't worry about it.'

Hugo looked confused, as though she had spoken in a foreign language.

'How was your day?' she added.

'My day? Mm, so-so,' he replied, rocking his hand. 'You?'

'Oh, you know, same old same old,' she said, not daring to look at him in case the guilt was written in her expression.

Instead, she switched channels to a wildlife documentary and stared at the television, not really interested in the programme, but it would do for now. She just hoped they wouldn't be showing any mating rituals. Her activities during the day should never have happened. How could she criticise her husband's behaviour when hers was no better? Mutual infidelity was hardly the way to save her marriage.

Hugo wasn't exactly the most sensitive man she'd ever met, but even he seemed to sense something was off. 'Is everything OK, Jane?'

She dared to give him a brief glance. 'Fine, why?'

'Just wondered. You're awfully . . . quiet,' he said.

Was that suspicion she could hear in his voice? She felt an overwhelming urge to confess her indiscretions and beg his forgiveness. 'I've just got a bit of a headache,' she said.

'Have you had a drink?'

'No I haven't!' she snapped, immediately regretting her temper. ' Sorry, but I'm allowed to have quiet moments like you do, aren't I?'

'OK, OK! Only asking. Is there any supper?' Hugo always

ate late; he was used to it.

'We've got smoked salmon,' she replied. 'I could make you a sandwich.'

'Fine. That will be great.' He followed her to the kitchen, fetched a bottle of cold white wine from the fridge and took a single glass from the backlit display cabinet.

'I'll have one too, if you don't mind,' she said.

He filled two glasses and took his into the lounge while Jane prepared the salmon. She had an artistic flair with food and could make even a plain snack look appetising. Triangular sandwiches and a garnish of sliced lemon and parsley made the simple supper look even more appealing. She carried the food into the lounge on a tray and set it down on the side table next to Hugo's chair.

Hugo had switched channels back to ITV and was watching the news intently, barely acknowledging her as she passed him the plate. As always, her husband liked being waited on, believing food tasted better when someone else prepared it. Sitting opposite Hugo, Jane sipped her wine and stared soulfully into the fire as the flames died down, turning to look at him only when he spoke.

'Is there anything wrong, Jane?' he asked, turning off the TV.

'Not really, no, but thanks for asking,' she replied, surprised that he would even notice. Was his concern prompted by consideration or suspicion? It was certainly unusual. Perhaps she had been underestimating him. After all, it was always she who he came home to, wasn't it? The dalliance with Jeff had been more than just satisfying, it had made her feel like a desirable woman again, but the man she really wished would desire her was her husband, not her window cleaner.

Hugo washed the last of the sandwiches down with the wine and smacked his lips. 'That was lovely. Thanks, Jane.' He looked at his watch. 'Early start tomorrow,' he said. 'I think I'll go up. Are you coming?'

Jane loaded the plate and glasses into the dishwasher and followed her husband upstairs.

When she reached to the bedroom, Hugo was cleaning his teeth in the en-suite bathroom. She quickly slipped into some sexy lingerie that flattered her figure and lay on the bed to wait for him. Although she had washed and changed the bedding after Jeff had left, she was convinced that Hugo would be able to tell what had been going on this mattress just a few hours earlier. Suddenly, she felt an overwhelming lust for Hugo. It was as if her own infidelity had somehow unleashed her inner seductress.

Jane stretched out like a cat on the bed, the silky sheets and smooth satin erotic against her skin. The bed was king size, opulent and luxurious, and she lay thinking of ways in which they could put it to best use.

Hugo finally emerged from the bathroom, swiping his right hand across his mouth and looking at her. He smiled and dimmed the lights. 'Well, hello,' he said, admiration in his voice. There's a sight for sore eyes. I take it your headache is better?'

She smiled, confident that he was no longer suspicious of anything. They kissed and caressed, eventually sharing their bodies with each other as they made love for the first time in months.

Afterwards, Jane lay for a while in semi-darkness, thinking

about what the future might hold as Hugo snored gently beside her. She was now more determined than ever to make the marriage work; she knew she had too much to lose if she were to walk away from it all – or if Hugo were to walk away from her. *I am not going to give this up without a fight*, she thought. She'd enjoyed her afternoon with Jeff more than she'd enjoyed anything for a long time, but she still loved Hugo, and twenty-five years of marriage counted for a lot more than a few hours of illicit sex, no matter how pleasurable it had been. When things were good between Jane and Hugo, they were very good, and that was how a marriage was meant to be.

Jane turned and cuddled into her husband's back. She was asleep within minutes.

19

Claire opened her eyes with a start, unsure for a moment where she was, before realising that the darkened room she was lying in was not her bedroom but her lounge. Sleeping upright on the sofa had left her with a stiff neck and, oddly, a raging thirst. She switched on the small table lamp next to her and looked at her watch. 'Ten o'clock! I must have been tired!' she muttered. The flat was silent, but she had the strange feeling that she had been awoken by some sort of disturbance. Richie, perhaps? He was supposed to have come round for a meal, wasn't he? He said he'd be there no later than eight, but surely he would have woken her when he arrived, not padded round the flat for two hours. As she went to get up, she thought she heard movement in the kitchen. She held her breath and her heart began to pound as she recalled Richie saying last week that he was worried about burglars.

She prayed that it was Richie she could hear, but dared not call out in case it wasn't. Her mind racing, she decided that the best course of action would be to turn off the lamp and remain as still as possible. The burglar – if it was a burglar – might not even have realised there was anyone home. Carefully, she turned to lie full length on the sofa with her back to the room. She was still wearing her navy blue uniform from work, and in the darkened space she would be practically invisible against the black leather.

She heard the kitchen door close, and then footsteps on the landing. Another door opened – one of the bedrooms or the bathroom, she couldn't tell which. Then there was the click of a light switch and a muted glow in the room that brightened and faded briefly as whoever was there opened one of the landing doors. That unnerved her. What if they switched the living-room light on next? They would surely see her if they did that, and then who knew what might happen?

It was quiet for a while longer, and then Claire heard the front door slam closed. She breathed a sigh of relief, then froze as she heard footsteps coming back up the stairs.

There was a loose floorboard just outside the lounge and Claire jumped as it creaked. She heard a man's voice say

'Hello?' and the room was suddenly flooded with light.

Claire knew there was little point in trying to avoid what was about to happen, but perhaps she could make it a little less bad. She turned over and sat up with her arms outstretched.

'Look,' she said. 'Just take what you want, but please don't hurt me. I'm a nurse, and there are people who depend on me to – Oh! It's you!'

Standing before her wearing a bemused expression was Tony Deakin, her landlord and the owner of Deakin's Antiques on the ground floor of the building.

'I must say, that's a very kind offer, Miss Frazer, but I think I have enough stock in my shop already.'

'I – I thought –'

'I've just finished my six-monthly stock take,' he went on before she could finish. As I was locking up, I noticed that your front door was wide open. I thought I'd better take a look to make sure you were all right. I'm sorry if I frightened you.'

Claire had regained her composure by now, and was more annoyed than scared. 'But that doesn't give you the right to go poking around in my flat, just because you're the landlord.

That's a violation of –'

'Woah, woah! What on earth are you talking about? All I did was walk straight up the staircase to this room and switch the light on. What sort of person do you think I am?' He looked genuinely affronted. 'I'm disappointed you would even consider that of me, Miss Frazer.'

Now that she thought about it, the idea that Tony Deakin would violate her privacy in that way was indeed ridiculous. Her landlord, who'd always had a soft spot for her, was one of nature's gentlemen, and wouldn't in a million years dream of doing what she had just accused him of.

'I'm sorry, Tony. I'm just a bit on edge. I could have sworn there was someone in the flat before you came in. The front door was wide open, you said?'

'That's right,' said Tony. 'You're lucky it was me. Anyone could have come in.' He thought for a moment. 'In fact, perhaps someone did. Would you like me to take a look round to make sure?'

'That would be such a relief, if you wouldn't mind,' she said.

Two minutes later he was back. 'There's no one here, and I can't see anything obvious, apart from it looks as though someone has ransacked your wardrobe in the bedroom.'

'Ah, yes, that's me, I'm afraid. I've been meaning to tidy up in there.'

'Good. Well, looks as though no harm done, then. You probably just didn't close the front door behind you properly when you came in,' said Tony. 'If you're OK, Claire, I'll be off. There's a nice steak-and-kidney pie with my name on it defrosting at home.'

Claire saw her landlord out. Now that she thought about it, she couldn't recall the solid thunk of the front door closing when she'd back-heeled it earlier on. It mustn't have caught properly. As she went back up to the kitchen to make herself a drink she started to shake with the realisation that anyone could have walked in, and how lucky it was that she had come to no harm. Had someone really been in the flat or had she imagined it? Perhaps that glow from the landing had just been a passing car's headlights. How could she have been so careless? She filled the kettle for tea and then, thinking better of it, poured herself a large brandy instead. Where was Richie? None of this would have happened if he'd come over like he was supposed to have done.

She took her brandy into the lounge and picked up the phone, tossing her hair back haughtily while waiting for him to answer. There was no reply from his landline. Perhaps he was in the car. She dialled the unfamiliar mobile number he'd given her and he picked up on the fourth ring.

'Hello?'

'It's me,' she replied.

'Hi, darling, what's up? You sound annoyed.'

'You were supposed to be at my place, remember?'

'Oh yeah, sorry about that, Claire, I was really looking forward to it,' he said.

She felt resentment overwhelm her. 'How can you be so selfish? One minute you're telling me you love me and want to whisk me off to Paris, the next you can't even be bothered to turn up to eat this lovely meal I've cooked for you. Well, too late. It's in the bin now!' Even in her present mental turmoil she knew she was being irrational, but the night's events had made her lose all control of her own emotions and she needed someone to blame other than herself. Her face crumpled as she pulled at her clothing, finally letting out a screech as tears rolled down her face to the corners of her mouth.

'I hope you have a bloody good reason, Richie!'

'Claire, I'm sorry, but you know how it is. The boys decided on a drink at the pub, and then Mr Richards said he was taking us all for a curry. I'm on my way home from there now. He's the chairman; I couldn't say no. I –'

Before he could continue, Claire dropped her bombshell. 'And while you were elbow deep in chicken Madras, I was being burgled!' she shouted.

'What?'

She stood in silence for a few seconds, letting her accusation sink in. Then her stomach turned as she stared at an empty space on the floor next to the sofa. 'Oh no! Those bastards have taken my handbag – it's got my bank cards in it, my purse . . . Oh, Richie, this is awful!'

So there *had* been an intruder. Her legs buckled beneath her and she collapsed onto the sofa with the phone in her lap.

'Listen, I'm coming over, Claire!' said Richie. 'Just sit tight.'

As she replaced the receiver, she noticed for the first time that the 'New Messages' light was flashing on the handset. She pressed 'Play' and heard Richie's voice.

Claire, baby, I'm so, so sorry, but I don't think I'm going to be able to make it over tonight. Mr Richards has told us he's got something planned for after the meeting. Whatever it is, it won't make up for not seeing you. I love you, darling. See you soon.

The message was timed at five forty-seven.

20

'Claire, sweetheart, are you OK?' asked Richie as soon as he arrived. 'I'll make us both a cup of tea. Just sit there, and I'll call the police. Are you OK?'

'Yeah,' she sniffled. 'Actually, I'll have a brandy, please. Large one.'

'Tea would be better, Claire, I think. Then I'll get the police,' he said, disappearing into the kitchen and returning a few minutes later with two steaming mugs. It seemed to Claire that Richie had no sense of urgency. Why didn't he phone the police first and then make the tea?

'OK, now tell me exactly what happened. Are you hurt? Did they threaten you?'

'No, I'm fine. Something woke me up and I heard someone in the flat.'

'Heard someone? You mean you didn't see them?' said Richie.

'No, but I was really scared, Richie. Then Mr Deakin from

downstairs came up to make sure I was OK.'

'Perhaps it was Mr Deakin you heard in the flat, then,' said Richie.

'I thought that too, but he got really upset when I asked him. Besides, he didn't come anywhere near the spot where my bag disappeared from after he switched the light on, and if he had taken it, why would he come back up? No, he's a nice man and I've known him a long time; I'm sure he was telling the truth.'

'How did he know to check on you? Did you call him?'

'No, he just . . . well, I, er . . . I didn't . . . I mean, he said he thought I mustn't have closed the door properly.'

'*What?*'

'Apparently, the front door was open, so he came in to see if I was OK. He looked round, but the burglar was gone.'

Richie dialled 999 and reported the theft. Claire stood by the window, watching the street as though the thief might still be there. Half an hour later a panda car pulled up outside. Claire was annoyed to see no flashing blue lights.

Two police officers emerged, one male and one female,

putting on their caps. Richie let them in. 'Good evening sir, madam,' said the man. 'I'm Sergeant Haines and this is WPC Blainey. Perhaps you could run me through what's occurred here while my colleague takes a look round,' he added, taking out his notebook.

Claire and Richie told Sergeant Haines what they could while the WPC wandered through the flat. As the interview was finishing, she returned to the lounge. The sergeant looked at her with an unspoken question and she shook her head. 'No, boss; no sign of a forced entry.'

Sergeant Haines closed his notebook with a snap. 'Right, sir,' he said. 'So, to summarise, your lady friend here came home from work, left the front door open and dozed off. When she woke up, some rascal had helped himself to her handbag, but didn't take anything else. Is that about right, madam?'

'Well, yes,' said Claire. 'Although when you put it like that –'

'And all that was of value in your bag was your cheque book and bank card?'

'My make-up wasn't cheap,' said Claire defiantly.

'So, if you contact your bank first thing,' he went on, ignoring her, 'they can freeze your account and you won't actually have been robbed of anything, will you?'

'Except her handbag, boss,' said WPC Blainey. 'I bet it was a nice one, eh, miss?'

Claire couldn't tell whether the officer was being sympathetic or sarcastic, so she said nothing. In fact, all her expensive handbags were in her wardrobe. She wouldn't have wasted one on work.

'So, Miss Frazer, it would seem there isn't really a great deal for us to do except to advise you to be a bit more careful in the future. It sounds as though you've had a lucky escape.'

'They won't have one if I catch them,' said Richie. 'I'll kill 'em.'

'I wouldn't advise it, sir,' said the sergeant. 'My colleague will leave you with details of counselling and victim support services –'

'I don't need that. I'm not upset,' snapped Claire, irritated, 'I'm bloody annoyed. I just wish you'd get my stuff back.'

'Sometimes these nasty experiences don't hit home until

the next morning,' said the WPC, handing Claire a sheaf of leaflets. 'We'll leave you with an incident reference number too, just in case the bag turns up somewhere, but, as I say, if you contact your bank in the morning there's not much else either of us needs to do.'

Claire's eyes welled up again, this time from frustration rather than fear. 'Oh God, I felt so tired when I got in from work that I just collapsed in a heap on the sofa. Why didn't I check the door?' she sobbed.

PC Blainey was sympathetic. 'It's not entirely your fault, love. Some scumbag took advantage of your mistake, that's all. Try and get some rest. We have the details now.' To Richie, she said, 'Are you staying with her?'

He nodded his head, looking rather dejected about the whole process.

Richie let the officers out. The street was bathed in a bright white light that made the trees along the pavement look incandescent. As he stood watching the police car pull away Claire walked up behind him and put her arms round his waist.

'Full moon,' she said.

'Yep. They say strange things happen on a full moon,' he replied. 'Especially after midnight. Mwaaaah.'

'Don't!' she punched his back good naturedly. 'Come on, let's get inside. It's cold and it's eerie out there,' said Claire.

For once, Claire was glad to have Richie sharing her bed. He lay on his back, his arm outstretched so that she could snuggle up and use his chest as a pillow. An owl hooted in the distance. Claire's eyes became heavy, and she began to nod off.

'Rich?' she said sleepily.

'Mmm?'

'I missed your message. Sorry I shouted at you earlier. I shouldn't have done it.'

He kissed her forehead in reply and lay staring at the ceiling as her breathing deepened towards sleep.

'No,' she heard him whisper as she drifted off, 'you shouldn't. But sorry doesn't always make it right.'

21

Brian had every other Saturday off, and Jinny, who didn't work weekends, made sure they took full advantage of the fortnightly opportunity to lie in. Since they'd decided to try for a baby their lie-ins had become more like love-ins, and Jinny had been pleased to find that her pregnancy had done nothing to reverse the trend.

She woke around nine o'clock and nudged Brian.

'It's Saturday!' she said. 'You know what that means.'

He opened his eyes slowly, stretching his arms above his head and yawning wide like a lion before grabbing Jinny in his arms and holding her against his chest. His body hair, which she adored him for, tickled her nose and she rubbed her face against him, breathing in his familiar masculine scent. He rolled over, making a playful growl, and began gently nibbling her neck, finally working his way round to her mouth and kissing her passionately.

If there was ever a perfect couple, thought Jinny, *it's us –*

each so accepting of the other and totally in love.

They aroused one another with increasing urgency until Jinny could wait no longer. She grabbed his face and stared into his eyes, 'God, you're a sexy beast,' she whispered. He kissed her from top to bottom before parting her legs to make love to her. As usual, they orgasmed simultaneously, the sensation so powerful it left them drained.

They lay in each other's arms for a while before Jinny sat up with a start.

'Brian! What time is it? We're meant to be meeting Claire and Richie for lunch at the Bell at one o'clock!'

'Don't panic, we'll be there,' replied Brian, who was hearing about the arrangement for the first time. 'We've got an hour yet.'

'An hour? Brian, that's nowhere near long enough for a girl to get ready! Phone Richie up and say we're going to be late.'

Jinny dashed off to shower as Brian left the bedroom. She emerged ten minutes later, frantically rubbing her hair dry, as he returned.

'Richie's just told me there was a burglary at Claire's flat on

Wednesday,' he said.

'Oh, yes. Claire was really shaken by it. She hasn't been to work for the past couple of days, trying to get over it. I meant to mention it to you last night, but you looked so done in after your training course that I thought you didn't need to hear any bad news. They came in while she was asleep, apparently. Took her handbag with all her bank stuff in. In a way, though, she was lucky. Anything might have happened, if you think about it.'

'Crumbs, that's dreadful!' said Brian. 'Anyway, I've said we'll see them at one thirty, so get your skates on.'

Half an hour later they were standing by the front door, ready to leave.

'See?' said Brian. 'We've got loads of time and you still look as beautiful as you always do.'

'Awww, you say the most lovely things, Brian. I'm so glad you're back.'

'Shall we walk it, love?' said Brian. 'It's a smashing day.'

As they strolled hand in hand, the autumn sun cast a beautiful light across the scene. It was the kind of light photographers and artists adore. 'Look how how pretty the chapel is in the sunlight, and the green fields surrounding it,' said Jinny. 'It's gorgeous, isn't it? We'll have the baby christened there.'

A short while later they arrived at the pub. Brian looked at his watch.

'I said we'd meet them outside. They'll be along soon. We're a few minutes early. In the meantime . . .

Brian pulled Jinny to him and kissed her passionately. 'You bring out the worst in me, you know,' he said jokingly.

There was the sound of a car horn and a shouted 'Put her down, Brian' from Richie as his Volvo pulled into the car park. As they walked towards their friends, Jinny noticed how tired Claire appeared, yet she'd still made sure she looked like a million dollars and oozed her usual sex appeal.

Brian and Richie went to the bar while the girls found a table. 'How are you now, Claire?' said Jinny. 'I still can't believe this has happened. It must have been awful.'

'It's not so much what they took – the bank was able to sort all that out on Thursday morning – it's the way it leaves you feeling violated. People don't realise how much trauma a break-in causes, and worry. I won't sleep without the light on now.'

Brian and Richie arrived with a tray of drinks. 'Here we go, girls.' They all chinked glasses together and the two men joined in the conversation about the burglary. 'Imagine how horrific it must be to have burglars in your house while you are actually in there,' said Richie. 'If I'd have been there, I would have given them a hiding!'

Claire rolled her eyes. 'But you weren't there, were you, love?' she said. 'You were in an Indian restaurant.'

Richie shifted uncomfortably. 'All right, all right, let's leave it at that, shall we? I did explain.'

Brian and Jinny exchanged a glance and a brief grimace.

'And the main thing is, you've lost nothing and come to no harm, have you?' said Richie.

Jinny felt she should intervene before their little digs became a full-blown row. 'Is it hot in here, or is it me?' she said, taking off the cardigan of her twinset.

'Actually,' replied Claire, removing her shawl to reveal a more than ample cleavage, 'it is a bit warm.'

Jinny looked across at Brian, expecting his eyes to be drawn irresistibly to the necklace that dangled between her friend's breasts like a hypnotist's pendulum, but he was merely studying the menu. Richie, who had clearly seen it all before, was looking at the specials board.

'I know what I'm having,' said Brian, and passed the menu to Richie.

Claire shuffled closer to see and he planted a kiss on her temple. 'Love you, babe,' he said.

Claire looked up at him and smiled. 'Love you more.'

Jinny, knowing Claire a little better than everyone else at the moment regarding her planned infidelity, was a little nauseated by Claire's shameless duplicity and tempted to ask Brian to have a word in Richie's ear, telling him to be careful. For all that she liked and admired Claire, a lot of her friend's behaviour quite frankly baffled and even disgusted her.

Brian was also watching the exchange. 'Looks like they've made up, then,' he muttered into Jinny's ear. Then, louder, 'What are you having, love?'

'Oh, I don't know. I'll have the same as you,' Jinny

answered, irritated by her friend's antics.

Richie noted their choices and went to the bar while the other three chatted. Jinny kept the conversation going. 'So, did you discover anything else missing from the flat after the police left?' she asked.

'No, that's the funny thing,' said Claire. 'Nothing else – only my handbag with all my personal stuff. I just can't believe it happened.'

'What are you going to do?' asked Jinny.

'Well, what would you suggest, Jinny?' Claire shot back, clearly irritated.

Brian intervened. 'Well, there's no point dwelling on it, is there? If it's gone, it's gone, whatever it was. Of course, I'd never ask what was in a lady's handbag, Claire,' he added with a smile, but if he'd been hoping to raise one from Claire he was disappointed.

Richie brought another tray of drinks and they all raised their glasses once again. 'Here's to the baby!' said Brian.

'Still not having any morning sickness yet?' asked Claire.

'No, thank goodness,' replied Jinny.

Brian smiled. 'She's doing fine,' he said, rubbing her tummy gently as he kissed her on the nose. Jinny was enjoying the shift in attention, but her smile evaporated when she saw who had just walked into the pub. This could spell trouble. Fortunately, the waitress arrived at that moment with their meals, and placed herself between them and the new arrivals.

Jinny felt the stiletto heel of one of Claire's knee-high leather boots tap her calf as the plates of food were placed on the table.

'What's the matter?' Claire whispered.

'Enjoy your meal!' said the young waitress, who then hurried back to the bar. The pub was getting very busy now. Claire nudged Jinny's calf again.

Jinny didn't want to say anything, and shook her head to avoid the subject. After all, it was awkward with their partners present.

The expression on Claire's face told Jinny that she was obviously not going to be satisfied with that, and as she finished her meal Jinny felt another kick as Claire shot her a meaningful look and excused herself to go to the ladies'. 'I should go too,' said Jinny a few seconds later, and rose from her seat.

Brian looked at Richie. 'Was it something we said?'

'Probably,' replied Richie. 'I can't do anything right for her lately.'

'Don't be silly,' said Jinny. 'You know us girls always go in pairs.'

Jinny hurried to the loo to find Claire waiting for her. 'Come on, then. Spill! What is it?' she said as soon as Jinny was inside.

'Hugo and Jane are here,' said Jinny.

'Hugo! Where?' replied Claire, sounding almost panic-stricken.

'Standing at the bar. You can see right across from there to where me and Brian are sitting. They're eventually going to notice us. That would be really –'

'Perfect,' said Claire.

'Perfect? How?' said Jinny.

'Because with Jane and me in the same room, he'll be able to see exactly what he's missing,' Claire replied, breaking into a smile. She stood in front of the mirror, straightening her skirt and hair. 'Come on, let's get back.'

Jinny followed, chewing her bottom lip and thinking how many ways this could go wrong.

Claire returned to her seat next to Richie. 'Shove up!' she said as she sat down, crossing her legs and lighting a cigarette.

Brian looked on disapprovingly as she tried to waft the smoke away from Jinny. 'Fancy another drink?' he asked.

'Yes, same again please, Brian,' replied Richie.

The girls passed their empty glasses, and Brian went off to order another tray of drinks. Claire moved into his seat, which was in full view of Hugo and Jane at the bar, but Hugo was deep in conversation with Jane. Claire watched, fixated, as Jinny tried to distract her. 'Aren't you afraid to be in the flat alone now, Claire?' she asked as Brian returned.

'Ugh! Not half!' replied Richie for her as he took the tray of drinks from Brian and laid it on the table. Claire looked at Richie disapprovingly, but he kept talking. 'You need to move in with me, Claire. Seriously, it would be much better.'

Jinny looked at Claire, interested to see what her reaction

to Richie's proposal would be.

Richie held Claire's drink out to her. 'Well?' he said.

'Thanks,' she said, taking it. 'Moving in is a big step, Rich. I'm not going to decide something like that over a pub lunch. Let me think about it, OK?'

'I think she's getting cold feet, Richie,' teased Jinny, hoping to provoke Claire into shifting her gaze from Hugo to her. Richie would surely notice soon.

All she received for her pains was a cold stare. Jinny quickly realised she had overstepped the mark.

This time it was Brian and Richie who got up to go to the loo before they left. They had been chatting about cricket, and Richie's attempt to demonstrate a sweep shot resulted in a glass crashing to the floor. Jane turned at the noise, noticed Claire and Jinny and waved. Hugo looked over too, and Jinny saw his face drain of colour. He turned to the barman to ask for another drink.

'Did you see that, Jinny?' asked Claire. 'He looked guilty, didn't he?'

'He certainly didn't look happy,' agreed Jinny. 'But what

does that prove?'

'There's only one reason he'd feel guilty – because he wants me more than her. And I'm going to make sure he gets exactly what he wants.'

22

As their blue Mercedes pulled up in the drive, Jane looked at Hugo, uncertain and frustrated. Since their resumption of conjugal relations the previous Wednesday their relationship had been better than she had known for a long time. Yes, Hugo had been somewhat preoccupied, but had explained that there were some tough decisions he had to make at work which were preying on his mind. His suggestion that they have lunch at the Bell had come as another welcome surprise. Saturday lunch out had been a regular treat for much of their married life but it, like so much else that was good, seemed to have fallen by the wayside. The highlight of her weekends now was a gossip with their cleaner, who came every Saturday morning to tidy the house. While they were ordering at the bar, though, his mood had changed as though someone had flicked a switch. They had eaten their meal almost in silence and left as soon as they had finished.

'What made you so edgy in the pub, Hugo?' she asked.

'Edgy? I don't know what you're talking about,' he said, opening his door.

'You seemed to change as soon as you saw those people from the hospital,' she added, careful to avoid naming Claire. 'What was all that about?'

'Jane! Maybe I would rather not see people from work on my days off – have you thought of that?'

'You don't seem to mind spending time with them in the social club after work,' she countered. 'Oh, forget it. I'm going in.' It looked as though the renaissance their marriage had been stillborn. There was clearly something going on in his department that Hugo didn't want Jane to find out about. The records section where she worked rarely crossed paths with Theatres, so he might not want Jane socialising with his own staff outside the hospital in case they started to compare notes. Little did he know that she and Claire were already friends! If Hugo wasn't going to tell her what was going on at work, then perhaps Claire would.

As Jane walked towards the house Hugo overtook her and opened the front door, going in first. He hung up his jacket, went into the lounge and sat down.

'Why must you always be so suspicious, Jane?' he asked as she followed him in.

'Why must you always act so suspiciously?'

'I've told you, I have some big decisions to make,' he said.

'Then tell me what they are. I might be able to help you.'

As Hugo opened his mouth to reply, the phone rang. 'I'll get it,' he said, leaping up from his chair.

'Saved by the bell,' muttered Jane as he lifted the handset.

'Hi, hi, how are you?' he said to their caller, his face breaking into a smile. 'Everything all right? Lovely to hear from you. Jane, it's Peter!' Hugo and their eldest son spoke for a short while before he handed her the receiver. Peter wasn't sure when he would be home next and, as usual, Jane reminded him to keep in touch. 'Try to be home for Christmas, darling,' she said. 'Love you. Bye.'

Hugo was banking up the open fire, adding a couple more logs to the cinders. He loosened his tie and opened the latest Dick Francis novel. Jane went to the hallway, looking at herself in the mirror and rearranging her hair a little. She examined her face more closely, checking for wrinkles and thinking she could do with a new hairdo.

She called in to Hugo, 'I think I'll do some baking today.'

'How about one of your fruit cakes?' he suggested. 'You're really good at those.'

Oh, so I'm good for something then, she thought. To be fair, she really did enjoy baking, and for the next couple of hours she was in her element while Hugo sat and read by the fire. Immersed in what she was doing, she was startled when a tap-tap-tap on the glass of the kitchen door broke her concentration.

'Yoo-hoo!' called Celia, opening the door and entering the room like a force 10 gale, flour rising from the work surface as she passed.

'Darling, I've been shopping, and I thought I'd call by,' she went on.

'Oh, lovely,' replied Jane, struggling to exude the same theatrical zest in return.

They exchanged kisses on each other's cheeks. 'Did you buy anything nice?' asked Jane.

'Absolutely! Have a look at this!' Celia held up a red-ochre silk blouse. 'Isn't it just me?'

'Um, mm, yes, it's lovely,' said Jane, who thought the colour wouldn't suit her Caribbean complexion at all.

'What's the matter, Jane?' asked Celia, slightly deflated. 'You don't sound so sure.'

Jane felt a tinge of guilt. 'No, it's fine. I just thought something a bit brighter would have been even better. I'm sure it will look great on you!'

Celia packed the blouse back into a bag marked *La Boutique d'Harvington*. 'As you can see, it's still my favourite shop,' she said with a cheeky wink and a smile. 'Jane, darling,' she went on, 'you can't beat a spot of retail therapy.' Celia chuckled. 'Anyway, what have you been up to?'

'Um, baking?' suggested Jane, looking around the kitchen, whose every surface seemed to be occupied by cakes or their ingredients.

'Mm, smells good,' said Celia.

'Hugo likes fruit cake, so I've made three. Hang your coat up and we'll have a slice with a cup of tea,' said Jane, filling the kettle.

Celia walked through the lounge to the hallway past Hugo sitting by the fireside. 'Hi, darling! It's only me,' Jane heard her call out.

Jane could imagine Hugo rolling his eyes to the ceiling. He'd often commented that her friend was loud enough to wake the dead, and was no doubt aggrieved at the shattered quietude of the afternoon. *Well, good,* thought Jane.

Celia returned to the kitchen and pulled out a stool. 'Have you heard from the boys?' she asked.

'Funny you should ask,' said Jane. 'Peter rang earlier today.'

'Oh, lovely!' said Celia. 'And how is he?'

'He sounds very happy – loving university.'

'And Stuart?'

'Yes, he's fine as well. All good. He wants to follow in his father's footsteps, but we'll see,' Jane added.

Celia looked genuinely pleased. 'You must both be so proud,' she said. 'Such lovely boys. George and I always wanted children, but it wasn't to be and now, of course, it's too late.'

Jane felt a twinge of sadness mixed with guilt as she was

reminded of how lucky she and Hugo were to have raised a family.

'And Stuart wants to be like his father,' added Celia. 'That's wonderful!'

'So long as he sticks to being a brilliant surgeon and leaves out the rest,' said Jane instinctively.

Celia looked worried as she made the tea. 'What do you mean, Jane? Are you two still having problems?'

'That's just it, Celia,' said Jane. 'I don't know. One minute he's all smiles and the next he's like a bear with a sore head. I do love him, but I'm not sure what he's thinking half the time. He says it's problems at work, but . . .'

'That will be it, then,' said Celia. 'Like I told you on Monday, I'm sure it's nothing to worry about. I think you're just feeling guilty because of your –' she looked towards the lounge before turning back to whisper '– *your window cleaner moment.*'

Jane flushed beetroot red. She hadn't told anyone about her romp with Jeff Glass. How had Celia found out? Celia wasn't the most discreet of people. If she knew, then so would –

'Perhaps you could get a job as a stripper,' Celia added, before bursting into gales of laughter.

'Could you two keep it down in there, please?' called Hugo. 'I'm trying to read.'

With relief, Jane realised Celia was referring to the inadvertent peep show she'd told her about on the phone, not her afternoon of infidelity.

'Shh!' she said, laughing herself now, before calling to Hugo, 'Come and get some tea and a slice of cake.'

'You're a very lucky man, Hugo,' said Celia as he came to fetch them. 'A wife who is both beautiful and a wonderful cook. You don't know how well off you are. You chose your woman well.'

'Ah, well, Celia, that's the thing,' he said. 'Life is full of choices. The trick is to make the right ones at the right time.'

23

It was three o'clock by the time Claire and Richie reached his house at Bowlers Green, a small village five miles south of Harvington. As they pulled up outside, he looked at the detached property and back at Claire. 'You know what I'm going to ask you,' he said.

'Yes, but the answer is still no,' she replied quickly.

'I knew you'd say that, Claire, but why? Come on. What's the point in paying Tony Deakin all that money every month when you could live here for free? I love you, Claire,' he insisted. 'What are you worried about?'

'I'm just not sure, that's all,' she told him. 'Moving in with someone's a big step. I'm happy with the way we are at the moment.'

'At the moment? How do you mean? Claire, you either want us to be together or you don't!' His response somehow sounded like an ultimatum.

'Let me think about it, Richie. I have a lot on my mind,'

she said, hoping this would be enough to mollify him.

That was true enough, at least. Richie was so besotted with her that she knew he would treat her like a queen if she pledged herself to him, but there was a huge complicating factor in the mix – Hugo Bowman. At any other time she would have jumped at the chance of snaring a lovestruck boyfriend with a big house and a well-paid job, but right now Richie had been relegated by Hugo to her Plan B. He stood no chance against a top surgeon who looked like a film star and earned a mega salary, but she needed to keep him dangling for a while longer in case her Plan A, which she had dubbed Operation Acquire Hugo, failed.

Richie huffed and puffed as he opened her door to let her out, but said no more. She knew this wouldn't be the last of it, though, which put her on edge. They walked to the house in silence, and as Richie put his key in the lock Claire said, 'Look, I'll go back to my place if it's easier.'

'Why?' he asked.

'Well, you don't seem happy about my decision.'

'No, well, I don't know, Claire. It's up to you,' he shrugged.

'I want us to be together, that's all. Is that so wrong?'

'No!' she replied, a little irritated.

'Well, what is it, then? We've been together for six months now. You've just been burgled. I want you to move in with me. It just seems like a good time to take things to the next level, don't you think?'

'Richie, I don't know what I want at the moment. I do love you, but . . .'

'But what?' he asked with raised eyebrows and surprise in his voice.

'I'm so used to being on my own,' she said, not entirely dishonestly, hoping he would accept the excuse. 'It has been working OK for us, honey, hasn't it?' she added.

She walked up to him and held him close, wishing he was Hugo.

'Come on,' he said, leading her towards the stairs.

She had succeeded in winning him round a bit too well, she realised.

'Actually, Richie, I'm a bit tired. I drank quite a bit at the Bell. Would you mind if took a nap on the sofa?' she asked.

He sighed. 'Go on, then. I'll watch *Grandstand* for an hour or so.' He switched on the TV, pulled her boots off as she lay down and kissed her at length before leaving her alone. She drifted off to the sound of a Rugby League commentary.

She woke to find the TV silent and the room dimly lit. She was lying beneath an eiderdown that Richie must have fetched from his bedroom to cover her with. She looked at her watch; it was seven o'clock.

Richie looked up from his chair, where he had been reading by lamplight. 'Ah, the sleeping beauty awakens,' he said with a grin.

Claire yawned widely. 'Make us a cuppa, Richie, would you please?' she said.

'I might,' he said, kneeling down by the sofa and stroking her head with his hands. 'What's it worth?' He pulled back the eiderdown and buried his head in her cleavage.

'Richie!' she hissed.

He looked up. 'Yes?'

'A cup of tea, please.' This time it was an order rather than a request.

He took her hand and placed it over the bulge in his trousers. 'This is the effect you have on me!'

She couldn't help but laugh as he stood up and headed for the kitchen. He was soon back with a tray of tea and some chocolate biscuits.

'Let's have an early night,' he suggested.

'An early night?'

'Mm, for a change, you know,' he said.

She knew only too well. Just a pity it wasn't Hugo making the suggestion.

'Richie, there's early and there's early. It's only seven o'clock for goodness' sake.'

He drained the last of his tea.

'OK, forget it. Let's go to the pub for a drink.'

'Um . . .'

'No?' said Richie, sounding exasperated now. 'Well, what *do* you want to do?'

'I know, how about we get a Chinese takeaway and rent a film?' she said. That would take up a good few hours, at least, during which she wouldn't have to think about putting him off either cohabitation or sex.

'Hallelujah!' Richie cried. 'A decision at last!'

'Right, get your coat quickly, before I go off the idea,' she said, and gave him a peck on the forehead.

As they drove through the winding country lanes, Claire jumped when a pair of bright eyes appeared in the darkness before them. He swerved the car, narrowly staying out of the ditch that bordered the road.

'Bloody foxes!' he moaned. 'They're everywhere!'

Ten minutes later they were standing in Harvington's Chinese takeaway, the Golden Palace, a far from palatial red-painted shop with bright yellow walls covered in oriental landscape pictures. A huge white ceramic Buddha with a very happy smiling face sat on the counter next to the till. Red and gold lanterns hung from the ceiling. Despite their pub lunch, the pervasive smell of Chinese food being cooked started their stomachs gurgling. Richie grabbed a menu and beckoned Claire to sit with him. As she sat down, she smiled at the round-faced Chinese lady behind the counter with her jet-black hair buffed up in a bun. It shone like gloss paint as she turned occasionally to speak to the cook on the other side of the dividing door streamers.

Richie placed their orders and paid. While they waited, the shop door opened and Len McClure and his assistant Iain practically fell into the shop. They had clearly been drinking all afternoon.

'Oh God, no,' Claire said under her breath, hoping they wouldn't notice she was present. Of course, they did.

Iain could not contain himself. 'Wey hey! Sister Claire! Hi, mate, sorry, I forget your name,' he said, holding out his hand for Richie to shake. 'Nice one,' added Iain looking at Claire and winking.

Claire felt Richie tense. 'Leave it,' she said under her breath. 'He's just a kid who's had a few too many.'

Len, who, though also drunk, was much better able to hold his beer, looked across and rolled his eyes. 'Please pardon my bibulous assistant, Sister. And Mister Sister,' he added, nodding at Richie before ordering for himself and Iain.

The Chinese lady was looking nervously at Iain, so Len grabbed his arm and led him to a bench. 'Sit down before you fall down,' he said.

The brown bag containing Claire and Richie's order arrived first and the woman read out its contents in a tuneful voice before handing it over the counter to Richie. They left with a quick goodbye, Richie shaking his head in disbelief.

'What a pair!' he said. 'Your life in their hands!' He tutted. 'I wouldn't want them anywhere near my operation, if ever I needed one.'

'I know what you mean,' replied Claire.

The made a swift diversion to Blockbusters for a video – 'Oh, Jinny told me about this one,' said Claire, choosing *The Woman in Red* – before returning to the car. While Richie concentrated on the driving, Claire sat deep in thought recalling the last time she'd been in a car at night, when Hugo had driven her home from the club on the night of Tim's birthday. She could still feel the passion of that magical kiss on her lips. Her stomach fluttered with excitement.

'Penny for them?' said Richie.

'What?' answered Claire, returning reluctantly to the present from the Hugo world she had drifted into.

'What are you thinking about?' he asked her.

'Nothing, really. The burglary, I think,' she answered, saying the first thing that came into her head. Immediately, she realised she had restarted the discussion she'd been trying so hard to avoid.

'Well, you know how I feel about that with you living alone there,' he said.

'Yes, I know,' she said. 'I told you I'd think about it, and I will.'

She couldn't face another argument. A quick change of subject was required. Then an idea struck her.

'Darling?' she interrupted him.

'What?'

'You know you said you wanted to take me to Paris?'

'Well, I said "somewhere" and you said "Paris",' he said with a smile, 'but yes, I remember.'

'Let's go next weekend,' she said.

It might be her only chance; the offer certainly wouldn't still be there if Operation Acquire Hugo succeeded.

24

Monday morning. Claire stirred once again to the unbearable buzzing of her alarm clock. She felt Richie stretch across to press the snooze button and remembered he had stayed the night. Plan B or not, she needed to keep him sweet for this week at least, with a visit to Paris on the horizon. She wrapped her arms around him and buried her head in the groove of his neck while he kissed her forehead tenderly. As she made to get out of bed, he playfully pulled her back. 'I would love to stay in bed all day with you,' he told her, holding her face in his hands and looking into her eyes as if he was trying to reach her soul. For a moment, she wondered why she didn't appreciate him more; he loved her too much, maybe. Maybe as much as she loved Hugo.

'I know, but . . . I must get ready.'

'Come on, Claire, what is it?' he asked, holding her firmly and clearly unwilling to release her until she gave him the reassurance of an answer. 'Don't say you're going off me; I can't bear the thought of losing you.'

She pulled away. She longed for the things a new relationship brings – passion, excitement, surprise. She longed for all that, and the more she endured Richie's attentions, the more she wished they were coming from Hugo. The mannerisms she had once found attractive in her boyfriend were now mere irritations to be coped with. The way he stirred his tea, the tales full of bad jokes he told to their friends to impress them when they were out, the way he snorted when he laughed – all these would make her long for Hugo desperately. She sometimes felt that she and Richie had little left in common, and six months was starting to feel like a lifetime. She knew she should have been flattered by his undying love, and, admittedly, he was great in bed, but she couldn't enjoy either the adoration or the sex while she was forever wishing he was someone else.

'Claire, you know how I feel about you,' he insisted. 'Seven o'clock on a Monday morning probably isn't the best time to talk about it, but, believe me, I've got something really special lined up for you in Paris next weekend.'

Claire took a deep breath and turned, running her fingers through his dark brown hair. 'You're so sweet, Rich, I do know that. It's just that sometimes I guess I don't know what I want. Even what's good for me. I'm so mixed up.'

'About what?' he asked her.

'I just need space sometimes to work it out,' she said.

The alarm clock buzzed again. Richie tensed. '*Fucking thing!* he raged, and thumped the button silent.

'You're right, Richie, this isn't the best time for this. Come on, let's get ready for work.' Work where Hugo was.

'Let's get ready for work!' he repeated sarcastically. 'How about we act like a normal couple and have breakfast first, then maybe a shower, and *then* we get ready for goddam work!' he shouted, throwing up his arms in frustration.

Claire took her clothes from the wardrobe and left the bedroom in silence to wash and dress in the bathroom. Richie called an apology through the bolted door, which she ignored. The longer she stayed angry, the less guilt she would feel. Richie didn't get annoyed with her often, but when he did so, it was usually in a big way. He had never laid a finger on her, but

221

she felt nevertheless that there was an undercurrent of violence in him not far below the surface. A Richie that she didn't know at all. It was the aspect of his character she found simultaneously most and least attractive. It certainly might be a useful trait if she were ever threatened. Every cloud and all that.

She went to the kitchen and made coffee, burning her mouth in her haste to drink it and get out of the house. Richie walked in wearing only his boxers. 'I'm sorry, sweetheart,' he said again. 'Friends?'

Claire noticed the time. 'Shit!' she hissed. 'I've got to go!' She poured the coffee dregs into the sink and ran to the stairs.

'Hold on! Hold on!' he called out. 'What about a kiss?'

She stopped halfway down and turned as he descended to meet her, giving him a quick peck before continuing.

'Lock up after you, honey,' she shouted. 'You've got a key!'

She shut the door firmly behind her and drove away from her problems into a new week.

***

It was eight o'clock when Claire pulled into the car park, and she should have already been in position and managing her team. She panicked a little as she checked herself in the mirror and reached across to her bag for her lipstick, just in case she should see Hugo. His NHS list was on Tuesday, but it wasn't unusual for him to be around outside his scheduled hours, either dealing with an emergency or popping in after his private work at the Lavender Clinic to see Tim.

She got out of the car and scanned the car park as she hurried to the main entrance. There was no sign of Hugo's royal blue Mercedes, she noted. She half walked, half jogged to Theatres and then, shoulders back and chest out, processed sedately down the corridor to her recovery unit. 'Hi everyone!' she called out with a false smile before throwing her bag down and making a U-turn towards Jinny's office.

Jinny looked at her wristwatch and purposefully at Claire. 'What time do you call this?' she asked, a pretentious expression on her face. 'You're meant to be the team leader. Some of us have been here since seven thirty!'

'Well, more fool you,' Claire shot back. 'Anyway, you're lucky I'm here at all, after what I've been through.' She felt like reminding Jinny that she was an office minion, not the matron, but decided against it. True, she could be a little overpowering at times, but Jinny really was worth her weight in gold, both as a ward clerk and a friend.

'I know,' said Jinny. 'I'm so glad you're feeling better now. I haven't mentioned to anyone about, you know, what happened. They think you've had a tummy bug.'

Typical, thought Claire, who had been looking forward to receiving a bit of sympathy from her colleagues. Still, she could soon put that right.

A theatre trolley could be heard clanging its way along the corridor towards the recovery room as Claire perused the morning's operating list. She watched as Lyn Hawes checked the patient in, and off they went.

'Oh well, better get started,' she sighed, putting the clipboard back on Jinny's desk, just out of her reach.

She walked into the recovery room. 'Hi! Who was working the weekend?' she asked Lyn, who was tending to her patient.

Lyn looked up. 'It was I.'

'Any problems? Anything I ought to know about?' asked Claire.

'Nothing major. There were a few fractures and later a stabbing involving some love triangle thing.'

Claire looked surprised. 'Really?' Perhaps the game she was playing might be more dangerous than she thought. If she ended up with Hugo, though, it would be worth the risk. With a shrug, she proceeded to check equipment supplies for recovery and the sluicing room.

Libby came in to tick off the first patient who had gone to theatre.

'Hi, Libby,' Claire called out.

'Hi! We missed you. Are you feeling better?' asked Libby. 'These bugs can really lay you low.'

Claire walked over to her. 'It wasn't a tummy bug,' she said quietly. 'That's just Jinny trying to be diplomatic.'

'Oh! What really happened, then?'

Claire's stomach churned for a moment, but she managed to keep her emotions in check. 'I actually got burgled on Wednesday,' she told Libby.

'Are you serious!' exclaimed Libby. 'When? What time?'

'Early evening. It wasn't even properly dark.'

'My God, Claire! Was Richie with you?' Libby asked.

'Well, that's just it. He wasn't with me; he was meant to be at mine but he went out with the boys from work, got drunk and went for an Indian. I was livid.' No harm bending the truth a little if, as she expected, she was about to dump Richie. When that happened, she wanted her staff to be on her side.

'You poor thing, Claire! I'm surprised you're even in this morning after going through that!'

'I know, but wait until you hear the rest,' she said to Libby.

'Go on,' said Libby.

'I was actually asleep in the living room, and I woke up to find them in the flat. Can you imagine it?' she asked in a low voice.

'Did they take much? *Did they hurt you?*

'No, but they could have. They stole my bag from right next to where I was sleeping. If I'd woken up then, they'd probably have killed me.'

'Claire, that is awful. Don't tell me any more. What did Richie say about it?' she asked as the next patient came into the recovery room. The pale blue air-conditioned room was

226

comfortable and soothing for recovering patients, although Claire found the colour clinical and cold. She and Libby looked on as Paula and Maria took the patient's pulse and made other observations.

Claire chewed her bottom lip momentarily and then told Libby, 'Actually, he wants me to move out of the flat and live with him.'

Libby looked down, arms folded, and edged her clog heel into the floor, deep in thought. 'And how do you feel about that?' she finally said.

Claire shrugged her shoulders. 'I don't know what to do. I'm not sure what I want, Libby.'

'You're going to have to settle down sometime, Claire.'

'Yes, I know, but it's not that simple. You see –'

At this point, Lyn called out, 'Can I have a hand, please? My patient can't breathe!' Every free member of staff responded, including Libby and Claire, and the patient was rolled into the recovery position quickly and treated successfully. Within seconds all was well, and then another patient entered the unit. The conversation would have to wait.

As they worked, Claire thought how differently she and Libby spent their weekends. Libby and Malcolm always seemed to be doing such interesting things together when he was on leave; certainly more interesting than a lunchtime booze-up and a Chinese takeaway.

During a brief lull in the recovery room, Claire took the opportunity to break for coffee. She walked down to Jinny's office for a chat.

'You look a bit cheesed off,' said Jinny.

'Just tired, really,' replied Claire.

'I'm not surprised, after your ordeal.'

Claire raised her eyebrows in agreement. 'Yeah, well. In fact, I could do with some annual leave.'

Jinny packed a wedge of paper into the printer. 'Why don't you book yourself a break then? You mentioned that Richie wanted to take you to Paris a while back.'

'Actually, we're going next weekend,' said Claire.

'There you are, then,' said Jinny. 'That's something to look forward to, isn't it? I'd so love it if Brian and I could ever afford to go there.'

'Yes, I suppose it is, but . . .'

Jinny frowned. 'But what?'

'Well, he said he had something really special lined up for me while we were there,' said Claire.

'And that's a bad thing because . . .' said Jinny, looking puzzled.

'Oh, Jinny, I think he's going to ask me to marry him.'

Jinny got down from her chair and actually jumped up and down before hugging her friend. 'Claire, that's brilliant! Oh, I'm so happy for you. Can I be your bridesmaid?'

'Jinny!' snapped Claire. 'For God's sake, calm down. You'll have the whole recovery room in here. Just because you want to live in a Mills and Boon story doesn't mean that I do. You know damn well who it is I want to be with, and it isn't Richie.'

'Well I'm sorry, Claire, but that's just silly. All right, it might be nice to have a little fantasy about your boss, but when someone as eligible as Richie is offering to marry you, you'd be stupid to give up that opportunity on what amounts to nothing more than a schoolgirl crush.'

Claire was taken aback a little by Jinny's forthright

response, not least because she knew it contained a good deal of sense. But Hugo, though . . . 'Oh I don't know,' Claire finally replied. 'It's so confusing, but you're right – things can't go on like this. Perhaps I've got it wrong and he isn't going to ask me that at all,' said Claire, more in hope than expectation. She felt under pressure to put a smile on her face. 'Anyway, time to get back,' she said as brightly as she could manage. 'Must pop to the loo first though.'

Claire stood in front of the locker-room mirror and looked at the pair of tired eyes staring back at her. The dark shadows underneath them made her both look and feel aged. All this wasn't doing her any good at all.

She quickly went to get her bag and touch up her make-up, but it seemed that the more she added to her tired skin, the worse it looked. In the end she decided to make do with giving her hair a good brush and a relacquering. She returned to the unit holding her cap, a little disappointed that Jinny seemed so dismissive of her feelings for Hugo. This was surely more than a schoolgirl crush. She looked behind her at Jinny as she crossed the threshold of the recovery room and almost collided with Hugo.

He caught her to stop her falling. 'We'll have to stop meeting like this, Sister,' he joked.

She laughed nervously at the old joke. Her face felt hot enough to ignite the fumes of his Aramis aftershave that were filling her nostrils.

'How are you?' he asked her.

'Fine. Yourself?' she replied.

'Seeing you has made my day,' he said.

'Thank you!' she said, looking round to see whether anyone was monitoring their exchange, before realising that nothing compromising had actually been said. This was just friendly banter; anything more was in her head. She hoped it was in his as well.

'By the way, I thought you looked super at the weekend,' Hugo said as he slapped the medical notes down on the admin desk.

Claire's temperature rose again. 'Thank you,' she repeated. 'And how was your meal at the Bell?'

He looked up. 'Oh, you know.'

What did he mean by that?

He stared at her for a moment and she felt her stomach doing somersaults. 'Do you fancy a drink later at the club?' he asked. 'Tim and I are going over. Why not join us?'

'Is it *your* birthday this week, then?' she asked.

'Ha ha, no, nothing special. Just an after-work wind-down,' Hugo explained.

'With or without partners?' asked Claire.

'That's up to you, Claire. Jane will be at an art class, I believe. Ask the other girls along too.'

She paused, looking at his blue eyes and his rugged visage. If she was honest, he wasn't exactly male-model material, but he had status and the swagger of success, both of which increased his sex appeal in Claire's eyes. There was definitely something about him that she was unable to resist. And if his comment last Wednesday about unfinished business was anything to go by, he felt the same way.

Before she could reply, she heard footsteps approaching and turned to find Rebecca Maine standing beside them with Hugo's Tuesday list. 'Perhaps I'll see you there, then,' she said, and with a 'Hi, Rebecca' went to check on the day's earlier emergency.

Claire thought back to how possessive her rival had been over Hugo's coffee the previous week. She recalled, too, the row in the corridor with Iain Stewart. Rebecca was a woman easily provoked into rage, and Len had mentioned that she was a martial arts expert. Claire would need to tread carefully there.

Claire passed on Hugo's invitation to drinks at the Liquor Clinic to the girls. 'Count me in,' said Paula. 'I'll definitely go if the top brass are buying. They earn ten times more than us!'

Claire had been hoping for an intimate evening with Hugo, or at least not too crowded a one, but to her dismay it seemed that virtually the whole recovery room was keen to take up his offer.

She would just have to make sure he gave her a lift home.

25

Even though her window wasn't lowered, Claire could still hear the Liquor Clinic's juke box from the passenger seat of Jinny's car as they pulled up outside. Jinny had reluctantly agreed to back up Claire's lie to Richie that tonight was ladies-only night at the club.

'Just so long as there won't be any strippers,' Richie had said when Jinny had called to pick Claire up, causing her face to turn bright red.

'Oh! Oh my goodness, no. I mean I wouldn't –'

'Relax, Jinny, I'm just kidding,' said Richie. 'I need to make some preparations for the weekend anyway. You girls go off and enjoy yourselves. You never know when you're going to get another chance. I'll ring you tomorrow, darling.' He kissed Claire on the cheek and walked towards his car.

'That was an odd thing to say,' said Jinny as Richie drove off.

'Oh, ignore him,' said Claire. 'With a bit of luck it soon

won't be any of his business what I'm doing, because I'll be doing it with Hugo.'

Despite sounding like a pop festival, the social club was only a quarter full and its usual fog of cigarette smoke was as yet just a light mist. Still, it was only half past seven, the night was young. Claire knew Libby and Malcolm wouldn't be there, but most of the other girls were likely to show their faces and liven the place up. It was never a flat evening when the theatre staff were out in force. Claire was dressed to impress as usual in a brown leather miniskirt, bomber jacket to match, and a cream boob tube showing nearly all of her stomach. Jinny had opted for her usual monochrome going-out scheme, choosing a white blouse over black trousers and stylish black boots.

As they walked into the club, there was a wolf whistle.

'Huh, here we go,' said Jinny under her breath.

'Piss off, Len,' said Claire, enjoying the attention and trying hard to keep a straight face.

Len was grinning like a Cheshire cat while holding his pint. He liked to be noticed almost as much as Claire, and was always ready for a joke and a wind-up. 'Steve!' he called out to the barman. 'Get these two lovely ladies a drink, my man.' He flung a ten-pound note on the bar. Then in came more of the staff, Rebecca Maine among them. 'Ay-up!' Len called out. 'Here comes the Karate Kid and her gang! You've seen the workers, and now here come the shirkers.'

Jinny raised her eyebrows. 'It's a good job nobody takes you seriously, Len, crikey!'

'Jinny,' he said, moving towards her, 'the day people start taking me seriously will be the day I leave. I mean it: if the folks I work with can't take a joke, that will be it for me.'

From the look on Rebecca Maine's face, Claire thought that day might arrive sooner than Len anticipated.

Over the next hour, the jukebox volume slowly rose and the atmosphere became a little more charged. Claire was feeling optimistic. 'I think it's going to be a good night tonight,' she said as she took a long draw on her cigarette.

'Yeah, I reckon,' replied Jinny, turning her head to avoid her friend's second-hand smoke. Claire stubbed out the cigarette, popped a stick of chewing gum in her mouth and shook her hair back as she scanned the room and straightened her clothing. 'What time is it?' she asked. 'Hugo and Tim should be here soon, shouldn't they.'

Jinny ignored the question. 'Is Richie going round to your place later tonight?' she asked.

'I hope not,' replied Claire. 'I said I'd see him in the week. Why?'

'Well, I was just wondering if . . .' Jinny paused.

'What?' insisted Claire.

'Nothing, it's OK,' said Jinny.

'No, go on,' insisted Claire.

'Well, I'm feeling guilty about lying to him earlier. If I thought that you and Mr Bowman were going to, you know, *take advantage*, with the flat being empty and everything . . .'

'Don't worry, Jinny, nothing's going to happen,' said Claire. 'I just fancied a night out on our own, that's all. I'm not looking for anything else.'

Whether Jinny believed the lie, Claire couldn't say and really didn't care, but her words seemed to mollify her friend.

'And just to say, if Steve has a lock-in, I'm not staying that late,' said Jinny.

'Don't worry, hun. If I do stay, I'll get a cab home, same as I did last week.'

Jinny shook her head, smiling. 'I don't know how you do it.'

Neither did Claire, but four vodka and limes later, she couldn't care less as Hugo and Tim arrived, heading for the bar. Hugo looked across and said something to Tim before coming over to them. 'What are you drinking, ladies?' he asked.

Claire's mouth opened, but nothing came out.

Jinny spoke for the two of them. 'One vodka and lime, one tonic water, please, Mr Bowman, thanks.'

'Coming up,' he said and returned to the bar. Jinny looked at Claire. 'Crikey, Claire, get a grip on yourself.' She chuckled. 'You're in a right pickle.'

Claire knocked back the last of her drink before turning to Jinny. 'This has never happened to me before, Jin. It's really . . . weird.'

'Just be careful, Claire,' Jinny told her friend.

'I know what I'm doing. Don't worry,' Claire insisted, regaining her composure.

'Just don't hurt anyone, that's all,' replied Jinny. 'Including yourself.'

Hugo and Tim brought the drinks across and sat with them. As much as the staff insisted they would never talk shop after hours, conversations inevitably started that way.

While they chatted and laughed, Claire noticed that Tim's eyes were drawn to her cleavage. He lifted his gaze to meet hers and winked. She immediately looked at Hugo, worried that he might think she was coming on to his registrar, but he was listening politely to Jinny as she expounded on the importance of accurate stock recording.

There was a commotion at the door as the rest of the recovery-room staff arrived – Lyn, Paula, Maria, Rhonda and the student, Amanda – together with a group of student nurses from Kingfisher Ward. All were in a party mood, no doubt having warmed up with pre-drinks in the nurses' quarters, and were pushing through the crowd to the bar. Even Paula, who was a Mormon and didn't drink, was laughing and joking.

There was a sudden cheer as a glass shattered on the floor behind the bar. Steve was having some difficulty dealing with the sudden influx of people, so Len went behind the bar to lend a hand.

The conversation turned to foreign travel, Hugo and Tim sharing stories about the countries they had visited and the strange cultures and often diabolical healthcare systems they had encountered.

'You're so lucky to have seen all those things,' said Jinny. 'I've never been anywhere. Claire's going to Paris with Richie this weekend, aren't you, Claire? That's so romantic. Ow!'

The exclamation was in response to a fierce kick from Claire's stiletto under the table. The last thing Claire wanted was to remind Hugo of her existing involvement.

'It's just a work thing,' she explained. 'I probably won't see anything of him after we get there. Might as well be spending a weekend in Cleethorpes.'

'I'm sure the good folk of Cleethorpes would welcome you with open arms,' said Hugo with a laugh.

Claire offered to get the next round of drinks, but Hugo insisted on paying. As he went to the bar, Claire tottered off to the ladies' while Jinny chatted to Tim. In some ways, she envied Jinny's ability to socialise with men. Whenever Claire was in conversation with a member of the opposite sex she usually felt as though she was being evaluated rather than listened to. 'That's the price you have to pay for being one of the beautiful people, I suppose,' she said to herself as she reapplied her make-up in the mirror.

Returning to the table, Claire threw her jacket off and lit another cigarette. Her blonde hair shone against her tanned shoulders. Hugo returned with the drinks and smiled at her appreciatively. The feeling was mutual. Hugo always looked good, the way Claire liked her men: black trousers, Armani belt, black jacket, Aramis aftershave, gold wristwatch. Regular foreign holidays had left him with a year-round tan that glowed against his white shirt. With his thick, wavy hair and rugged looks he oozed virility, charm and, of course, sex appeal.

By ten o'clock, the club was quite busy, and the smoky atmosphere somehow made it feel cosy.

'So, where's your partner tonight?' he asked. 'Richie, isn't it?'

'He's doing his own thing,' she replied, shrugging her

shoulders. 'We're not joined at the hip,' she continued. 'We like to go out on our own sometimes. He has his own place and I have my flat.' She was having to shout over the music.

He nodded. 'Seems like a good arrangement,' he said.

'It works for us,' she said. She leaned over and murmured into his ear, 'It means I can let my hair down once in a while.'

He smiled as he sipped his drink. Claire flicked her heels off and ran her well-pedicured foot up and down his trouser leg. Hugo remained composed and the four-way conversation continued as she played footsie with him under the table.

There was quite a party atmosphere in the club, frequently punctuated by Len's raucous laughter as he stood among a group of ward staff exchanging rude jokes that left little to the imagination. Hugo looked over at Jinny, who was trying to stifle a yawn while holding her hand over her mouth.

'Are we keeping you up?' he asked. Tim and Hugo both laughed.

'Sorry, I think it's because I'm . . . I'm working too hard,' she said.

'And a very good job you do too,' said Hugo.

'Thanks,' said Jinny. 'It's nice to be appreciated. I just feel so knackered lately. What time is it, anyway?' she asked.

Claire's eyes popped open. 'Oh, come on, don't be a party pooper!'

Jinny's reply was drowned out by an ear-splitting clangour as Steve gave the bell a good shaking and called out last orders from the bar.

It took around half an hour for the crowd to dwindle down to the usual suspects, while Steve circled the tables shouting, 'Glasses, please! Can I have your glasses, *please*!'

Tim turned to look at Len, who was in his habitual spot propping up the bar. He walked over and returned a few seconds later to confirm a lock-in. Steve closed the curtains and turned the jukebox volume down, pushing a few coins in to keep the music playing.

'I'm locking up now,' he said. 'Is anyone else leaving?'

Jinny stood up to put her jacket on. 'Sorry, everyone, I'm done. And Brian will be worrying if I'm not home soon.'

Claire and Jinny hugged and said their goodbyes and Steve locked the door behind her. Claire, deciding another check on her make-up and hair was required, made a further trip to the ladies' loo, quite literally when her heel caught in a loose piece of carpet and she half-staggered her way across the dance floor. 'Bloody hell, Claire!' shouted Len. 'I didn't know you could foxtrot!'

'Oh, there's a lot you don't know about me, Len,' she replied.

She returned and sat down heavily next to Hugo, who seemed very pleased to welcome her into his presence. Tim seemed to sense that three was a crowd, and excused himself to join the company at the bar. Claire lit another cigarette and sipped her drink, then sucked slowly on the slice of lemon it contained, never taking her eyes from his.

'Um, what you were saying about unfinished business . . .' she said.

'Claire, I think you've perhaps had enough to drink, don't you?' he said.

'Maybe, maybe not,' she said, taking another sip of her vodka and finally putting the glass down. 'But if you're trying to suggest I'm too drunk to know what I'm doing, then you're wrong.'

He gently placed his fingers over her wrist and then cupped her hands in his, looking deep into her eyes. 'You really do want this, don't you?' he asked.

'Yes, I really do,' she replied. 'And I know you do too.'

'What man wouldn't?' he said.

'There you are, then.' She smiled. 'Resistance is futile.'

'Jane will be back from her art class by now,' he said.

'We can go to my flat.'

'You sure that's OK?'

'Absolutely,' said Claire. 'Who's to know?'

'Steve, can you open the door, please?' called Hugo. 'I'm giving Sister Frazer a lift home.'

'As long as that's all you're giving her, eh?' shouted Len, to a smattering of laughter.

Steve unbolted the door to let them both out and slammed it firmly shut behind them. Hugo walked Claire to his car and took both her hands in his, the two of them staring into each other's eyes. 'You are the most beautiful woman I've ever met,' he told her.

They kissed hungrily, pulling apart only for air.

'Come on, let me take you home,' he said, urgency in his voice. 'If you're sure –'

'Oh, I'm sure,' she said, slightly out of breath.

He aimed his car keys and at the Mercedes, which looked as black as a hearse in the darkness. The parking lights flashed and he opened the door for her. He started the engine and leaned across to kiss her briefly before driving off in the direction of Well Street. As she sank back into the luxurious leather upholstery the catch phrase of a popular TV show kept running through her mind.

I love it when a plan comes together.

26

When they pulled up outside Deakin's Antiques, Claire was relieved to see that the flat was in darkness. She was also relieved that she wouldn't be going in there alone, being still unnerved by the previous week's burglary. They kissed before getting out.

'Let's go,' she said, swinging her feet onto the pavement. She opened the front door and led Hugo up the stairs to the landing. She quickly checked all the rooms to make sure there were no burglars and, most importantly, no Richie.

Hugo looked on, a little bemused. 'Everything OK?' he said.

'Perfect,' said Claire, going to the kitchen and filling the kettle.

Hugo followed her, putting his car keys on the worktop and his arms round her waist.

'Coffee?' she asked him.

'Please,' he answered. They stood locked together as the

water heated to boiling point.

'Nice place you've got here,' he said as he released her.

'Not bad, I suppose,' she replied, stirring the coffee. 'I could do with somewhere better, really.' She handed him a mug and began to flirt again. 'So, what is a rich big-shot like you doing standing here in this poky little flat with me?' she said, grinning and hoping for some flattery in return. She stood with her arms folded, waiting for his reply.

He leant against the door jamb, studying her from top to bottom, and then he began walking towards her. 'Come here, you!' he said as he pulled her close to his chest. 'You know why I'm here. We both know.'

'Do we?' she teased.

'I like you a lot, Claire, and I know you feel the same way about me,' he told her.

'Let's get comfy,' she said, going into the lounge and sitting on the sofa with her arms spread wide. 'Do you want to put some music on?'

He picked an ABBA cassette and turned down the volume. 'Don't want to wake the neighbours, do we?' he said, coming to sit beside her.

They kissed for a while, then Claire pulled away. For her plan to truly come together, she would need to separate Hugo from his wife. She already had a good idea of Jane's reservations about their marriage; here was an ideal opportunity to find out whether they were mutual.

'So,' she said. 'Your other half?'

'Jane? What about her?'

There was a pause as she looked into his blue eyes. 'Well, where does she think you are right now, for example?' she asked him.

He shrugged his shoulders. 'Work?'

'Work! Ha! At one in the morning? I don't think so, do you?'

'She probably guesses I'm at the club having a lock-in. It's hardly unusual.'

'Mm, that's plausible,' Claire decided.

'Anyway, who cares?' he added. 'She knows I like my social life. I work hard and I play hard. What's wrong with that?'

'You've got kids, though, haven't you? How about them?'

'What, are you writing a book or something?' he asked, grinning.

'I'm just interested, that's all,' she said. 'Sorry.'

He pulled her closer. 'Don't apologise,' he told her, lifting her chin. 'The boys are both at university now. There's only me and Jane in the house. We're like you and Richie, both doing our own thing.' He looked into her eyes. 'So,' he said, 'is the interrogation over now?'

She smiled. She was mesmerised by him, and it was obvious how attracted he was to her. Their lips touched, and suddenly they were both writhing on the sofa, immersed in and oblivious of anything but each other's body.

Claire was far from inexperienced, but she had never felt the passion and sheer ecstasy that Hugo's lovemaking aroused in her. This was more than just sex for her, and she sensed it was the same for Hugo. Afterwards, as they lay exhausted, she realised that she had passed the point of no return. If these meetings were going to be a regular thing between the two of them, she didn't see how she could possibly lead a double life with Richie still in it. It would have to be all or nothing – no

Richie and no Jane. Easier said than done, she knew, as she played in her mind various scenarios that might make her dreams reality. He stroked her head as they kissed more. She decided the finer details would have to wait – she was bound to come up with something. With a sigh, she cuddled into him and they were soon both asleep.

She woke to find Hugo hopping around the room in a frenzy, frantically doing up his trousers. 'It's five o'clock!' he said. Claire, who had never seen him look anything other than self-assured, couldn't help smiling at the undignified display of panic.

'Calm down! There was a lock-in, and everyone lost track of the time,' she suggested. 'Simple!'

He buttoned his shirt, then unbuttoned it as he realised the buttons were in the wrong holes. 'Nothing's that simple with Jane,' he said.

Claire pulled her boob tube up over her chest and her skirt down from her waist. From what Jane had told her, this couldn't be the first time he had stayed out till dawn, or even not returned home at all after a night out. Perhaps their marriage wasn't in quite as bad a state as she'd imagined. That could be a worry.

She went into the kitchen and filled a pint glass with water; her mouth had never felt so dry. He called out a hurried goodbye as he grabbed his car keys from the worktop. She spluttered on the last drop as she tried to respond to him. 'You go. I'll see you during the list,' she coughed.

He gave her one last hug before he left and she followed him down, standing in the doorway to absorb the fresh air. It was dark outside, and the night was still. An owl hooted. She wondered if it was the same one she had heard the previous Wednesday. Her whole world seemed to have changed since then. Her thoughts were interrupted by the sound of Hugo's engine starting. She watched the Mercedes until its taillights disappeared into the distance.

Claire decided that, since she would have to be up in less than two hours, it was hardly worth going to bed. Instead she showered and then made herself a fried breakfast to soak up the alcohol from the night before.

The first objective of Operation Acquire Hugo had been

achieved. Now she had to plan Operation Remove Jane.

27

Jane reached across the bed to find an empty space beside her. She sighed and lay on her back, staring at the ceiling. Outside, she heard the electronic whirring of the milkman's float followed by the clinking of bottles as he replaced their empties with two pints of silver top. Then came the throatier sound of a petrol engine approaching as a car pulled into the driveway. She got up and pushed the curtain aside to stare down at the top of her husband's head as he got out of the car and pushed the door quietly closed, stepping back as he looked up at the bedroom window before entering the house. She heard the kettle boiling and the soft chink of spoon on china. Then footsteps on the stairs and the hiss of the guest shower. When the sound stopped, she got up herself and got into their own en-suite shower. She went downstairs to find Hugo sitting in the lounge in his dressing gown, eating croissants and listening to the *Today* programme on the radio.

'Busy night? Lost your watch, did you?' she called out as

she walked past the lounge doorway to the kitchen, her cream dressing gown flowing behind her. Even Hugo didn't usually take the liberty of staying out until gone five in the morning. At least he hadn't tried to creep into bed and pretend he'd been there all night. She wondered what excuse he would come up with instead.

Hugo sighed. 'I know. I'm sorry.' He was quiet for a moment – probably concocting some fictitious emergency, she imagined. What he said next came as something of a surprise. 'There was a lock-in at the social club. I stayed behind with some people we hadn't seen for ages, catching up with each other. Before we knew it, it was three a.m. Then Steve threw us out. We were all hungry, so we decided to drive up the motorway to the services for something to eat.'

'Oh!' she said. That sounded plausible, at least, or was it just that she wanted to believe him? 'It's your list today, though, isn't it? I wonder what your patients would say if they knew their surgeon had been up all night.'

'There's nothing on it that Tim can't manage. He was the sensible one – went home early. I'll grab a couple of hours' sleep and go in later. How was your art class?'

'Great! It was a life class and the male model was a body-builder. Plenty of muscle definition to work with. It made me quite nostalgic,' she said. 'He took me for for a drink afterwards. Anyway, I'd better get ready. I work on Tuesdays, remember?' Jane didn't like telling lies, but that one had been worth it just to see the look on her husband's face.

By the time she was dressed and ready, it was seven thirty. She rushed into the conservatory to collect an umbrella, leaving a waft behind her of a scent that she knew full well he hated because it made him feel nauseous.

'Aren't you having any breakfast?' he said as she shrugged on her coat.

'I fancy a fry-up at the hospital canteen,' she said. 'I don't know why, but I feel famished this morning.'

28

Claire took a taxi to work, feeling too tired to drive and a little chilly. She headed for the recovery unit, hoping the day would go fairly quickly.

Jinny saw her walking by and called out, 'Blimey! Did you wet the bed or something?'

Claire gave her a discreet V sign and a sarcastic glare as she narrowed her eyes. 'I'll be over in a moment. Just let me show my face to the staff.'

Jinny gave her the thumbs up and then proceeded to check the lists for the day.

Claire took a deep breath and pasted a smile on her face before entering the unit with an enthusiastic. 'Hi, girls!'

There was a chorused response from all four: Libby, Rhonda, Maria and Lyn. Claire noticed they were one member of staff down.

'Where's Paula this morning?'

They all looked at each other and then back to Claire.

Libby piped up, 'Late, maybe?'

'She's not usually,' said Claire, looking at her watch. 'We'll wait another twenty minutes, and if she's not in by eight thirty, give her a ring.'

They continued their checks as Libby gave the orders. Claire looked on with her arms folded. She was both proud of and grateful for Libby – so efficient, and a well-trusted person to lean on whenever she felt the need to. Yet sometimes Claire also envied Libby's calm authority that could make her appear more capable of running the unit than she was herself. A stranger would probably have thought that she rather than Claire was in charge, even though Libby had never tried to give that impression.

The staff certainly had respect for Claire, who knew knew her job from back to front, and during training sessions students would be captivated by her maverick approach that could teach them more in a single memorable off-the-wall session than a whole week of book learning. Claire loved the attention and was proud of it, but she knew she'd find life much harder without Libby's old-school approach keeping things on track.

Claire scrutinised the lists and Libby joined her. 'How was the club last night?' she asked.

'Yeah, good,' replied Claire with raised eyebrows, wondering how she was going to get through the shift.

Libby's expression put Claire in mind of her old headmistress. 'I don't know how you do it,' she said.

'You're the second person who's said that to me in less than twelve hours,' said Claire.

'Burning the candle at both ends!' said Libby. 'I'm ready for my bed by ten o'clock these days.'

'That's cos you're old and past it,' said Claire.

'Past it? I'll give you a run for your money any day of the week, madam!'

Rhonda looked on from one of the oxygen bays as Libby pretended to take a swipe at Claire with the clipboard holding the list. Claire ducked and took a couple of steps back, laughing.

'Help!' Claire cried. 'Assault on duty! Whatever next!' Then she remembered her missing SEN and checked her watch.

'We'd better ring Paula to see if she's OK,' she said.

'Paula is off sick,' said Jinny, who had just entered the room. There was a silence as she walked toward the admin desk. 'Paula is off sick, isn't she?' she repeated, staring hard at Rhonda, whose face by now resembled a red-hot poker. Her ginger hair merely added to the impression: Claire could practically feel the heat just by looking at her. 'She phoned earlier.' said Jinny. 'She's got a hangover.'

'A hangover?' said Claire and Libby together. 'But that's impossible; Paula doesn't drink,' Claire added.

'No,' said Jinny. 'But apparently *someone* – she looked at Rhonda again – thought it would be a good idea to spike her drink. She's been sick as a dog all night.'

'What's the big deal? I only did it for a laugh,' said Rhonda.

Claire and Libby looked at each other and then back at Rhonda. 'How stupid are you?' asked Claire. 'Paula's a Mormon; it's against her religion!'

'All right, don't go on about it. I thought people were just saying she was thick,' she protested.

'That's a moron,' said Claire. 'There's only one moron in

this department, and I'm looking at her now. If were weren't one down, I'd suspend you. As it is, you can just do Paula's work as well as your own. Now get out of my sight!' she shouted.

Libby looked at Claire and frowned. 'Everything all right, Claire? I don't think I've ever seen you like this,' she said.

'I've got enough going on in my head at the moment without having to worry about someone poisoning one of my girls,' said Claire.

From the corridor, the clanging of a trolley heralded the arrival the day's first patient to the department. 'OK, girls, we have a customer. Let's get rolling,' Claire ordered. Lyn went to check the patient's wristband details and Claire wandered over to Jinny.

'You look like something the cat dragged in,' said Jinny. 'I suppose you were up half the night.'

'Thanks very much,' said Claire. 'But Jinny, let me tell you about what Hugo –'

'Claire, I really haven't got time for one of your lurid stories. I've got work to do,' she snapped.

'What? I haven't said a thing yet!' replied Claire.

'And when you do, it will all be about you, won't it?' said Jinny.

'Jinny, this isn't like you. What's the matter?'

'If you must know, my morning sickness has started and I feel bloody awful, so do excuse me if I don't feel like listening to you droning on about your love life. I've got more grown-up things to worry about.' She turned and stalked away to her office.

Claire walked back into the unit and sat at the admin desk, lost in thought as the shift bustled on around her. It seemed that everything was a bit off-kilter today, as though everything was slightly out of sync. Claire desperately wanted to tell Jinny about last night with Hugo, but it seemed she'd have to abandon the idea for now.

Claire's mouth was still dry from the previous day's alcohol, and when she looked in her make-up mirror the whites of her eyes – usually so clear and youthful – were bloodshot. She'd been looking forward to seeing Hugo at some point, but she didn't want him to see her like this. By mid-morning, though, she was feeling more like herself and decided to seek him out. She hadn't seen him within the short interval of the orthopaedic list, and she knew Tim was leading this morning, so hopefully she could get him on his own. She wandered into the medics' room to find it very quiet, with not even a hint of anyone having been in there. That was odd, Rebecca Maine would usually have been in there by now.

Claire decided to annoy Rebecca by setting up the coffee machine herself, ready for the end of the lists. Closing the door behind her, she went to the kitchen for water. As she returned to the medics' room she noticed that the door was now ajar. From inside, she could hear Hugo's and Tim's voices, lowered in conversation. Not wanting to interrupt a private discussion, she was about to return to the kitchen when something Tim said stopped her in her tracks.

'Hugo, are you sure about this?' he asked.

'As sure as I've been about anything, Tim. I'm telling you, I can't get her out of my head.'

Claire padded up to the door and put her ear to the gap.

'No offence, Hugo, but she's hardly the first nurse to have

caught your fancy.'

'Guilty as charged, Tim, and I know what you mean, but this one's different. Entirely unlike anyone I've ever met before. I've been obsessed with her for weeks. I've tried every distraction I can think of, but nothing has worked. And then last night . . .'

'Last night what?' said Tim.

'Well, let's just say that last night something happened that made up my mind once and for all. I'm going to leave Jane.'

Claire's heart was pounding so hard that she was sure the two men would hear it. She could hardly believe her ears. It seemed that Operation Remove Jane was going to be achieved without a shot being fired.

29

Claire's mind whirled with possibilities as the morning dragged on. By one o'clock the staff were getting ready to take their lunch breaks. The phones hadn't stopped for most of the shift, and Claire rolled her eyes as Jinny put her head round the door and made a 'phone-call-for-you' gesture. Wearily, Clare followed her to her office.

'It's Richie,' Jinny said.

'Richie? What does he want?' said Claire.

Jinny shrugged her shoulders and returned to her desk, in a hurry to organise the afternoon lists.

It was unusual for Richie to call her at work. Surely he couldn't have found out about last night. Could he? Victory might be in sight, but she couldn't afford to burn her bridges with her Plan B just yet. And certainly not before he'd taken her to Paris. Claire picked up the receiver with her stomach churning. Doubt was gnawing at her, but she knew she had to sound calm and confident. 'Hi, babes!' she said. 'Is anything the matter?'

'No, no. Just wanted to hear the sound of your voice, that's all. How have you been?'

'Since you saw me on Sunday, you mean? Fine!' Now that the doubt had gone, she could afford to feel annoyed at the interruption. She was overwhelmed by a feeling of tiredness once again as Richie droned on about the office and his workmates until it bored her to tears. Fifteen minutes later she couldn't care less whether he was picking up negative vibes over the phone or not. It was always the same boring crap.

She managed to break the monotony at last when he stopped talking briefly to cough. 'Listen, babe,' she said, 'I've got to get off now. A lot going on here.'

'Oh, OK, yeah. Er, listen. Why don't I come over to your place tonight?'

She hesitated.

'Come on,' he insisted. 'Put your feet up and relax a little. Have a cosy night in. Say, six-thirtyish?'

Claire knew how Richie liked their cosy nights in to end. She'd really been hoping to avoid his romantic attentions until the weekend at least, if possible.

'I'm not sure, love. I've had a busy day, and I was going to wash my hair and have an early night. You want me looking good for Paris, don't you?'

He wasn't accepting no for an answer. 'Oh, come on, Claire. There's plenty of time for that. Besides, you always look like you just stepped off a catwalk,' he replied.

Not today, I don't, she thought. 'Richie, trust me, I will not be good company. I am absolutely knackered.'

'Don't be daft. Look, I have to go. I'll see you tonight, six thirty, seven o'clock. I'll get us a Chinese,' he said, and hung up before she could refuse. Claire pulled a face at the handset before putting it back on the base and stood leaning against the desk. 'Fuck!' She spat the word out with immense irritation.

Jinny looked at Claire's blotchy red face. 'Starting to get complicated now, is it?' she asked.

'What are you talking about? I'm fine,' said Claire huffily.

'Really?' Jinny replied, reaching for the bag containing her packed lunch. 'I wouldn't like to see you when there's something wrong.'

'What's that supposed to mean, Jinny?'

'Do you really want me to say?'

Claire hesitated for a moment, then said, 'Actually, yes, I would.' Suddenly Claire felt a little light-headed as the energy drained from her. She really couldn't face any more today. She was dog tired.

Jinny pulled up a chair. 'Sit down before you collapse, Claire love. You look really pale. Have you had anything to eat today?'

Claire lowered herself to the chair. 'I had breakfast, but it was about seven hours ago.' She felt like a schoolgirl summoned to the headmistress's office.

'Eat this,' Jinny passed her a sausage roll. 'Don't take offence, Claire, but I'm getting worried about you at the moment. You know, drinking in the club till all hours and turning up here exhausted. This is affecting your work.'

Despite Jinny's disclaimer, Claire was offended. 'Hold on a minute!' she said, spraying flaky pastry crumbs. 'I can make my own choices, thank you very much.'

'Claire, listen for a minute. I'm your friend; just hear what

I'm saying. This thing with Hugo –'

'Shh!' Claire hissed. 'Someone's coming.' Claire had heard footsteps approaching, and they sounded familiar. Libby's sensible shoes. For all her good qualities, her deputy's air of authority and imposing presence could be a little intimidating at times. Like her husband, Malcolm, she had been in the services and it showed.

'Just off to lunch, Claire, if that's OK?' said Libby. 'Hi, Jinny.'

Claire nodded her assent and turned to Jinny again. 'You were saying?'

Jinny continued. 'OK, I'm afraid your work will suffer if you keep this up with Hugo, and you will most probably get hurt also. You're a good nurse, a really good nurse, but the way you treat Richie is appalling.'

Claire knew Jinny was right, but that didn't make her observation any more palatable. 'Hang on! Since when did you become an agony aunt? What's Richie and me got to do with you?'

Jinny shifted awkwardly. 'It's not just about you and Richie, though, is it? There's Mr Bowman's wife, for a start.'

'Jane? No, I'm sorry, Jinny, if Jane Bowman can't keep her man interested that's hardly my fault, is it? Anyway, there might not even be a me and Richie for much longer,' said Claire. She hadn't meant to mention anything about what she'd overheard, but Jinny's moralising was getting on her nerves now.

'Do you really think Hugo will be prepared to jeopardise everything he has?' asked Jinny.

Claire took the opportunity to backpedal. 'I haven't really thought about it, Jinny. I'm having fun. What's wrong with that? I'm not expecting him to leave his wife. I know what I said about loving him, but I'm not stupid. Two people can have a fling, can't they? It happens all the time.' If Hugo really was going to leave Jane there was no point in letting the cat out of the bag yet. Jane might find out and then who knew what could happen? Better to play it down for now. Claire could just imagine Jinny's face when the truth came out. It would be a picture . . .

'A bit risky, though,' said Jinny, dragging her back to the

present. 'Affairs usually end badly, one way or another.'

'Let me worry about that. You just stick to being a Stepford Wife.' Jinny's eyes filled with tears and Claire realised she might have overstepped the mark. 'Anyway, I'm going for lunch,' she said. 'Do you want me to bring you something back from the canteen?'

'No, don't put yourself out for me,' said Jinny.

'Suit yourself,' said Claire with a shrug.

As she strode to the canteen Claire reflected that arguing with Jinny was like kicking a kitten. Easy to do, but it didn't make you feel any better afterwards. 'Oh no!' she said as she entered the canteen and saw Jane Bowman standing by the cold-food counter, waving her over. As if the day hadn't given her enough to think about already. Hugo's wife, usually a cheerful companion, had a vexed expression on her face today.

'Beef salad roll, please. And a slice of cheesecake,' she said as Claire joined her. 'Thank you!' She fired the acknowledgement like an accusation as she added the items to the can of Coke on her tray.

Jane was clearly troubled, but, after her exchange with

Jinny, Claire couldn't face any more grief, since her bad mood was bound to be connected with Hugo's overnight absence. Perhaps she should just grab something cold and eat it in her car.

'Oh, Claire, am I glad to see you,' said Jane. 'I really need some good advice.'

She hadn't been expecting that. This could be an enlightening conversation.

'Same for me, please,' said Claire to the server, following Jane to the till and then to a table that had just become vacant.

'So, how are things?' asked Claire obligingly.

'Not good,' said Jane as she snapped open her Coke can. Throwing back her hair, she went into a rant about how Hugo had rolled in with the milkman that morning, how they rarely saw each other these days, how he was always 'working late'.

Though not the object of Jane's suspicion, Claire felt uneasy none the less. 'That's awful! Poor you, Jane,' she said sympathetically.

'I just don't know where I am with him, Claire,' Jane went on. 'Last week, I thought we'd turned a corner, but it looks like he's up to his old tricks again. I wonder where he would have gone, Claire. Who he could have been with.' Jane's neck and chest were becoming more hot and blotched the more distressed she became.

Claire was feeling rather uncomfortable herself, but she couldn't leave. They had only just sat down.

'He gave me some cock-and-bull tale about meeting up with old friends,' said Jane, 'but the more I think about it, the less I believe it.' She stabbed her cheesecake with a fork. 'This morning I found myself making up a story about fancying a body builder, just to make him jealous, for God's sake!'

That was useful information. If Hugo's resolve to leave her ever wavered, she could say she'd seen Jane with her fantasy date. 'I don't know what to say, Jane. I'm so sorry. This must be dreadful for you,' replied a delighted Claire with what she hoped was a convincing display of compassion.

'Thanks, Claire. I've heard rumours about him and his theatre nurse. Do you know if there's anything in them?'

'Rebecca Maine, you mean? No, I don't think so.' Claire didn't see the point of adding to Jane's suspicions by confirming them. If Jane threatened to throw him out then Hugo's male pride might just make him decide to stay. Things were already complicated enough as it was. Besides, Rebecca was out of the picture now. Judging by what she had overheard him say to Tim, Hugo was about to become a one-woman man. Her one-woman man. 'Maybe work is getting to him at the moment, you know? Perhaps he needs a break or something,' she added.

'Well, he did say he was having to make some tough decisions at work,' agreed Jane. 'A break might be a good idea. You and your chap are going to Paris for the weekend, aren't you? Perhaps we could come along with you two?'

Claire practically choked on her beef salad roll. Jane stood and patted her back. 'Are you all right, dear?'

'Yes, I'm fine,' said Claire once she'd recovered. 'But I'm sure Richie said that Paris flight is fully booked.'

30

Claire was asleep on her bed when she was disturbed by the sound of Richie's key in the door. The bedside clock showed seven p.m. She closed her eyes and feigned sleep as his footsteps came up the stairs. She felt him kneel by the bedside and could imagine him staring at her, then his hand stroked her hair gently before he planted a kiss on her lips. She stirred and opened her eyes slowly, moaning a little before acknowledging he was there.

'Knackered,' she whispered.

'Shh,' he replied. 'Just rest.' He lay down beside her and held her close in his arms. She could feel that he was eager for sex, but he must surely realise she wouldn't be feeling amorous right now. To be honest, after Hugo, she wasn't bothered if she and Richie never had sex again. If she could just put him off until she was sure Plan A had worked . . .

At eight thirty the phone rang. Richie was no doubt hoping for Claire to wake, which she did, but she kept her eyes closed. When the caller eventually gave up she heard him sigh and leave the bedroom. Her sleep might have been feigned but her tiredness wasn't, and she was soon dozing again. Then there was a sudden light and he was shaking her awake. She stirred and slowly opened her eyes.

'Hi, babe,' he said to her as she blinked until she got her bearings.

'What time is it?' she asked.

'Nine thirty.'

'Oof!' she said and stretched every limb of her body like a cat, followed by a huge sigh. 'I needed that sleep.'

'Obviously. Why are you so tired today?' he asked.

'Oh, don't you start!' she replied gruffly, suddenly feeling the pressure for an explanation. 'I've had nothing but questions all day.'

'OK, OK, calm down. I'll get you a coffee, shall I? Wake you up a bit.'

She lay back down and thought of the last time she had been in this bed, and how she wished the man she'd been with then were here now. She began to daydream about her future with Hugo: expensive restaurants, winter holidays in the alps. Had he left Jane yet? Perhaps that had been him on the phone, begging her to run away with him. No, she reasoned, probably not. After all, you couldn't end twenty-odd years of married life overnight, could you? There would be things to sort out, arrangements to be made. That would take a couple of days. By the weekend, though, Hugo would be a free man, she was sure of it.

'Here you go, sleepyhead,' said Richie, setting down a large mug of coffee beside her. 'Are you hungry?' he asked her. 'I'll have to heat up the Chinese in the microwave.'

Claire's stomach turned. That just about summed up her choices: après ski with Hugo or reheated Chinese with Richie. She was suddenly tempted to confess everything. It would break his heart, of course, but telling him would be the kindest thing to do in the long run, even if it meant missing out on a trip to Paris. She might be selfish but she didn't like to think she was cruel. Then again, her new life with Hugo wasn't exactly a done deal yet. She should at least wait until he told her officially. If she acted rashly now, she could end up with nothing. A bird in the hand . . . She gave Richie a sheepish smile.

'Thanks, Rich. Sorry if I was a bit off earlier. It really has been a pig of a day.'

'It's not the first time, though, is it, Claire? Sometimes I feel like I don't know where I am with you. You know how nuts I am about you, don't you?'

'I know, Richie. And I do appreciate it, but sometimes I just need a bit of space.'

'Are you getting fed up of me, is that it? Is there someone else, because if there is –'

He was getting a bit too close to the truth now. 'What sort of person do you think I am, Richie?' said Claire, choosing attack as the best form of defence. 'If I was going off with someone else, I'd tell you, wouldn't I?' *And with a bit of luck, I'll soon be able to.*

'So we're all right, then?'

'Yes, Richie, we're all right. Look, I'm really busy at work at the moment. I told you I'd be poor company tonight, and now you know why. We're going away at the weekend, aren't we?'

'I hope so,' said Richie. 'I wasn't sure if you still wanted to.'

'Just let me have these couple of days to myself, and I'll see you on Friday, all dressed up and raring to go, I promise.'

He was quiet for a moment and stood with his arms folded, thinking. 'So you're not suggesting we split up? Because I want this weekend to be really special. I can't wait for it to arrive.'

'Oh, nor can I, Richie,' Claire said. That, at least, was the truth. 'Just a couple of days,' she added, 'and it will all be sorted. Just go home for now.'

As she heard the front door close behind him, the phone rang again.

Could it be Hugo? Surely not.

It wasn't.

'Hi,' said Jinny. 'You in a better mood now?'

'I'm all over the place, Jinny.'

'Stay there, I'll come round.'

Ten minutes later they were sitting together on the settee as Claire brought Jinny up to date. She left nothing out, and by the time she had finished she felt as though a great weight had been lifted from her shoulders.

'Thanks for listening, Jinny; I know I can trust you not to tell anyone. I feel so much better now. I think I've literally unburdened myself.'

Jinny, though, looked as though she had just acquired a whole new set of problems.

'I knew you weren't telling me everything,' said Jinny. 'But now that you have, I wish you hadn't.'

'What do you mean?' asked Claire. 'This is fantastic!'

'Breaking up a marriage isn't something to be proud of, Claire. And what about Richie?'

'All good things must come to an end, Jinny. Besides, I really want this, you know that. Can't you just be happy for me?'

'I want you to be happy, Claire, of course I do, but –'

'Are you hungry, Jin? I'm starving. There's some Chinese in the kitchen. I'll heat it up.'

31

On Wednesday morning, Claire arrived at the hospital early, well rested and eager to throw herself into her work. The sound of ABBA was blaring from the car as she swung it into a parking space and switched the cassette player off. Looking into the vanity mirror, she flicked her blonde locks into place and checked her teeth for lipstick before getting out of the car.

Within minutes she was in the recovery room and ready to start the daily checks on equipment and controlled drugs. The girls came in one at a time, each registering her surprise at Claire's almost unprecedented punctuality.

Some bickering could be heard in the distance from the theatre staff – nothing on the scale of the previous week's ruckus but again involving Iain Stewart and Rebecca Maine. Len was on the scene playing referee, which only made the situation worse at first, but then Danny Edwards, the anaesthetist, arrived and resolved matters with various imprecations to stay cool and chill out.

Claire wondered whether Rebecca had received some news from Hugo that had put her in a bad mood. If so, she hoped that he'd confined their conversation to 'It's over' rather than naming names. If Rebecca knew that Hugo was leaving Jane for Claire, the next few days were going to be very awkward indeed.

'Thank God!' Jinny said from behind the admin desk after the row had died down. 'Welcome to the kindergarten.'

Claire walked across to her. 'Talking about kindergartens,' she said in a low voice, 'isn't it time you let the staff know about your little bump?'

Jinny blushed. 'I'll do it when I'm ready!' she replied, raising her eyebrows at Claire. 'We all have our secrets to keep, don't we?'

'Fair point. I'm still not sure what to do about this Paris weekend away.'

'You're not still thinking of going, are you? You've got to tell Richie about Hugo. It's only fair,' protested Jinny.

'I'm not telling him anything until I know for sure that Hugo has left Jane.'

'But you said Richie's going to propose, Claire!'

'I said I thought he might. He just said he had something special for me. Still, it wouldn't surprise me if it was a ring.'

'And what are you going to say if he does ask you to marry him?' Jinny stood with folded arms, waiting for a response.

'Oh, I don't know, Jin. I'll just have to cross that bridge if I come to it. Stop being so negative, will you?'

'I think you're crazy,' said Jinny. 'Honestly, Claire, since you set your sights on Hugo, you've had your head in the clouds. You're risking everything, and gambling your future on – what? An overheard snatch of conversation in the medics' room. If you're not careful, you'll end up on your own.'

'Maybe I like taking risks,' said Claire, but if she was honest with herself, Jinny was right. What if she'd misheard, or somehow got the wrong impression? She could really do with some confirmation.

At lunch in the canteen with Libby, Claire spotted Hugo on another table, deep in conversation with Tim Dawson. He looked over and gave her a distracted smile before returning to his discussion. Her stomach churned with butterflies, as it always did when she saw him. Hugo made a point and Tim looked over at Claire. Were they discussing her? She longed to go over and ask Hugo when they could be together, but since she wasn't even supposed to know that he was leaving Jane she could hardly do that. Besides, what excuse could she give Libby?

Claire went to the counter to refill her tea. By the time she returned, Hugo and Tim had left. She and Libby finished up and were returning to the recovery room when she saw Hugo outside Theatre 1, talking with Len. He noticed Claire and signalled he would ring her. Len looked from Hugo to Claire and winked, a lascivious grin on his face.

'What was that about?' asked Libby.

'Um, I'd left a message with Mr Bowman's secretary, asking him to call me about next week's list,' said Claire, thinking on her feet. 'Ignore Len; you know what he's like.'

She turned to smile back at Hugo but all she could see was his receding back as he moved off down the corridor.

Claire drove home, none the wiser than when she'd arrived at work that morning. The uncertainty was torture; she had to do something.

The flat still smelled of last night's Chinese. Claire threw off her coat and sat down. She got up and paced the room. She crossed to the telephone, lifted the handset, replaced it, lifted it again, took a deep breath and dialled.

'Hello?'

'Jane, hi, it's Claire,' she said brightly.

Had Hugo told his wife about her? She was going to find out soon enough. She closed her eyes in anticipation of the storm of invective she might have unleashed.

'Claire, darling, how are you? Looking forward to the weekend?' said Jane.

Claire let out the breath she'd been holding. 'Yes. Should be good,' she said. 'Jane, I was hoping we could have a catch-up. I was wondering if things were any better between you and Hugo.'

'Oh, Claire, don't ask,' said Jane. 'I don't know where I am with him half the time.'

'Shall I come round?' asked Claire.

'That's sweet of you, Claire, but I'm going to the ballet

tonight with my friend Celia.'

So, he definitely hadn't told her yet. Was he ever going to?

'Maybe tomorrow, then?' offered Claire.

'Actually, Hugo has asked if I could keep tomorrow night free. He said we need to have a talk. Very mysterious. Perhaps he's seen the error of his ways at last,' said Jane.

'Perhaps,' said Claire.

'I'm working at the hospital tomorrow, though,' said Jane. 'We could have lunch.'

'Great,' said Claire, trying to keep the excitement out of her voice. Tomorrow was D-Day, then. Or should that be H-Day? Whichever it was, in a little over twenty-four hours' time, Claire would have her man.

***

'The beef stew's good,' said Jane to Claire as they queued for the lunch counter on Thursday.

'I need to watch my figure, though,' said Claire, opting for a ham salad.

'Ha! I should be so lucky,' said Jane.

They paid and found a free table. Claire had been worried

that Hugo might see them, but according to Jinny he was doing private work all day.

'So, it sounds like you have an intriguing evening coming up,' said Claire.

'Sounds like it,' agreed Jane. 'I wish he'd just said what he wants to talk about, though. I don't like all this cloak-and-dagger stuff. It puts me on edge.' Jane moved the food around on her plate, but hadn't yet taken a mouthful.

'Jane, you know you said you thought Hugo was having an affair,' said Claire, choosing her words carefully.

'With his theatre nurse, yes,' said Jane.

'If you found out that was true, what would you do?'

'I dread to think,' said Jane.

'No, seriously. I mean, would you throw him out, scratch her eyes out or what?'

'I'm not exactly the violent type, Claire. To be honest, I've just about had enough. I don't think our marriage could take another blow like that, and I'm not sure I could either.'

***

'You did *what?*' said Jinny incredulously as they were drinking their afternoon coffee.

'I had lunch with Jane Bowman,' said Claire.

'The woman whose husband you're planning to run off with? God, Claire, you've got some front!'

'I needed to know what she's likely to do when he tells her about us tonight,' said Claire. 'From what she said, it doesn't look like she's going to put up much of a fight. In fact, I think she'll be pleased to be out of it. I'm doing her a favour really.'

Jinny was about to reply when the phone rang.

'Theatre clerk, can I help you? Oh, hello, Mr Bowman. Yes. Yes, she's standing next to me, actually. I'll pass you over.' She handed the phone to Claire. 'I'll give you some privacy,' she whispered and walked out of the office.

'Hello?'

'Hello, Claire,' said Hugo. 'I'm sorry I haven't been able to call before now. I've had . . . well, I've had quite a lot to think about this week.'

'You're not the only one,' she replied.

'Ha ha, yes, I can imagine,' he joked, although his voice sounded strained. 'Look, Claire, this isn't really something I wanted to discuss with you over the phone, but what happened between us the other night has made me really reconsider my marriage and my future. This might come as a surprise to you, Claire, but I . . . well, I . . .'

'Hugo, it's all right. I know what you're going to say,' said Claire. 'I have a confession myself. I was outside the door when you were talking to Tim on Tuesday. I know how you feel about me and I know about you leaving Jane.'

'Yes, I'm going to tell her tonight. This hasn't been an easy decision for me you know, Claire. Twenty-five years and two children creates a lot of history.'

'Don't look back, Hugo, look forward.'

'You're right, I know. It's so good that you're in my corner.'

Claire's heart was pounding once again. This was actually happening!

'What do you think will happen tonight, when you tell Jane?' asked Claire. 'I don't think she'll take it well.'

'I didn't think you knew each other,' said Hugo.

'Well, no, we don't,' said Claire, wondering how she could have been so careless as to let that slip. 'I mean, I don't think any wife would take it well.'

'Oh, I see. As it happens, you're right. Jane's been a little fragile lately, and I think she drinks too much. I don't want to drop a bombshell like that on her and just walk out. There's no telling what she might do. I'll sleep in the spare room tonight, just to be sure she's OK. I owe her that much.'

'Of course, Hugo,' said Claire.

'You're so understanding, Claire.'

'What is there to understand? When two people have so strong an attraction . . .'

'We really are on the same wavelength, Claire, aren't we?

'And after tonight?' asked Claire.

'I've booked a room at Harvington Manor for a few days. This has all been a bit sudden. I don't know how things will pan out, exactly, but the main thing is for the two of us to make a fresh start together. The details can be worked out afterwards. Claire, look, I've got to go. Thanks so much. Tonight will be a lot easier now.'

'Hugo, I love you.'

But the line had gone dead.

Jinny, who had been waiting in the corridor, walked back in as Claire replaced the receiver.

'Well?' she said.

'He's going to do it, Jinny. He's leaving her. He's booked us into Harvington Manor. It will be like a sort of honeymoon. How romantic is that?'

'It would be a lot more romantic if he wasn't married,' said Jinny, but Claire was already mentally packing her suitcase.

32

Claire had previously booked Friday off to give her time to prepare for the Paris trip. She rose happy and breakfasted quickly before hitting the shops. Harvington Manor was a five-star country-house hotel, and she would need to be dressed appropriately. She came back three hours and one maxed-out credit card later, dumped her purchases on the bed and set out for the hairdresser's, returning to the flat suitably coiffured at one thirty p.m.

The message light on her phone was blinking, but it was just Richie, telling her not to be late. He was supposed to be picking her up at six for their evening flight, but she planned to be gone well before then. She couldn't face the thought of the row that would inevitably follow if she dumped him face to face. No, she'd leave him a note: *It's not you, babe, it's me.* That would do. She was aching to hear from Hugo, but he probably had enough on his plate today, she reasoned, and she would be seeing him soon enough anyway.

She walked from room to room, wondering whether she would ever sleep there again. The flat had served her well, and Tony Deakin had been a considerate landlord, but Claire had always known she was destined for better. She thought about the house in Springfields that had been shared until today by Hugo and Jane. She'd never been inside, of course, but she remembered the developer's brochures that had littered the town when the estate was being built. Perhaps she rather than Jane would soon be wafting up that elegant staircase to their master bedroom with luxury en-suite.

She tried on her purchases, thinking about the most suitable occasion for each outfit as she removed the tags. Hugo would need a well-turned-out partner on his arm whenever he attended a function and she was determined not to let him down.

She glanced at her watch. Five o'clock! She'd been daydreaming for too long. She hurriedly packed her things and headed downstairs. As the front door slammed behind her she realised that she hadn't left Richie a note. Never mind, he'd find out soon enough.

***

Jane Bowman was feeling rather less confident about her future as she sat at her dining table, pen in hand, and thought back to the previous evening. In her heart of hearts she'd known what was coming, and she'd taken a sort of masochistic pleasure in watching Hugo squirm and prevaricate as he built up the courage to give her the bad news. When he'd finally told her he was leaving, it came almost as a relief. At least she would be spared the regular torment of wondering what he was up to and with whom.

She had to confess some surprise, too. His previous dalliances had, she was sure, never been serious. Hugo was someone who liked an easy life outside his job to offset the intense pressure he worked under. Easy relationships, too, while continuing to enjoy the comforts of home. Leaving her was going to cost him some effort. She wondered whether he would find the grass on the other side of the fence to be as green as he thought it was.

She was upset, yes, devastated, even, but surprisingly rather calm, all things considered. She supposed she had been expecting this day to come eventually, and had long ago decided what she would do when it arrived. She had questions, of course. That morning she had tried calling Claire Frazer in the hope of getting some answers, but there had been no reply. She hadn't bothered to leave a message. What difference would it make to know where it had all gone wrong?

She sighed and drained the last of the brandy she had opened that lunch time. The full bottle of tranquillisers next to it would have to be washed down with something else. She pulled her writing pad towards her. Top-quality vellum. Might as well go out with a flourish. She removed the cap from the Parker fountain pen Hugo had bought her for Christmas and began to write.

To whom it may concern . . .

33

Harvington Manor was set in twenty-five acres of rolling countryside and had earned its reputation during a century of providing top-quality accommodation for the elite. Claire was relieved to see Hugo's Mercedes in the car park opposite the gravelled entrance driveway. She squeezed her Mini Cooper between a Bentley and a Jaguar. The luggage could wait until later. No doubt the place had porters to do the fetching and carrying.

The majestic hotel was the perfect setting for a romantic break, as good as Paris, if not better. And, of course, she'd be sleeping beside Hugo rather than Richie. Claire mounted the marble steps and entered the grand building.

Inside there was an air of silent opulence. There were no porters around, just the odd chambermaid passing by. A smartly uniformed receptionist was arranging a vase of fresh, sweet-smelling flowers whose bright colours reflected in the highly polished walnut desk.

'May I help you, madam?'

'Yes – I'm . . .' She wondered how Hugo had signed them into the hotel. Was the room in his name or would they be Mr and Mrs? And, if they were, Mr and Mrs what? Smith? Bowman?

'Madam?' said the receptionist.

'I'm here to see Mr Bowman,' Claire said, crossing her fingers and hoping for the best.

The receptionist opened a large leather-bound ledger and ran her finger down a list of names.

'Bowman, Bowman . . . ah, yes, here we are. Mr and Mrs Bowman. Room 201. Second floor.'

So, Hugo had used his real name. That was good. He was clearly committed to making that fresh start he'd mentioned.

The receptionist picked up her phone. 'Would you like me to call ahead and tell Mr Bowman you're here?'

'No need for that,' said Claire. 'He's expecting me.'

As she waited for the lift, Claire felt a small pang of guilt that she would be taking Jane's name for the next few days, but she supposed it wasn't the done thing for a couple to flaunt their unmarried status in an establishment as traditional as this one. Besides, Bowman would be her legal name before long.

The lift transported her effortlessly to the second floor. The doors glided open with a discreet 'ting'. On the wall opposite the lift were a series of brass arrows etched with room numbers. Room 201 was to the right, a few steps down the expensively carpeted corridor. Her heart racing, she knocked on the door.

***

Jinny got home to be greeted by the tantalising smell of beef stew and dumplings. Brian loved cooking and usually prepared something delicious on Fridays, when he left work at four. 'You're home early!' he said as she kicked her shoes off and hung up her coat. They kissed as she entered the kitchen.

'Mm, that smells absolutely gorgeous, darling,' she told him.

'Come on, rest your legs,' he suggested. 'Glass of Guinness to keep your strength up? I've put some in the stew, too.'

He handed her a full glass, closed the curtains and dimmed the lights to create a cosy ambience. The stereo was already playing softly in the background.

'Right,' he said. 'I'll call you when it's ready. Don't move.'

'Fine by me,' she said, smiling. 'What's the occasion? Have I missed something?'

'No, we're having a cosy evening in, that's all, away from rubbish and politics and affairs. Because what you told me yesterday about the way Claire is carrying on made me realise how lucky we are to have what we have.'

'We are, aren't we?'

'Yes. And because you're so special, and you're having our baby, and I love you so much,' he said, planting a kiss on her lips between each phrase.

During the meal, they discussed baby names.

'I think Alistair if it's a boy,' said Brian.

'Or Alexander,' added Jinny between mouthfuls.

'And for a girl, Emily, Sarah – maybe Megan?'

Jinny pulled a face. 'Mm, Megan? Not sure about that one. Sounds Welsh.'

'And what's wrong with that?' he said.

She looked at him with loving eyes. 'You can't wait for this baby, can you?' she told him.

'I can. I'm just excited, that's all,' he said. 'I'm so glad I'm not Richie. This breakup with Claire has really knocked him for six.'

'How do you know that? I didn't think Claire had even told him,' said Jinny.

'She hadn't. The poor bugger rang here not long before you got home. So far as he knew, they were still going to Paris this weekend. He'd gone round to Claire's an hour early to pick her up and found the place deserted. Not even a note to explain. He was phoning here to ask if we knew where she was. He thought she'd had an accident or something.'

'And what did you say?' asked Jinny.

'What could I say? I told him what you'd told me last night.'

'What, everything?'

'He deserves to know the truth, Jinny. Claire might be your friend, but the way she carries on is disgusting. To be honest, I don't know why you two are so pally. You're worth ten of her.'

Jinny was never one to blow her own trumpet, but even she

was beginning to suspect Brian might be right.

**

'Come in!' called Hugo.

Claire opened the oak-panelled door to Room 201 and entered. She had never seen anything so luxurious except in a magazine. On one side was a huge four-poster bed that looked as though it would swallow you up if you dared to lie on it. Opposite that was a writing desk-cum-dressing table flanked by two armchairs upholstered in gold brocade. In the far corner was a huge TV; thirty-six inches, at least, Claire judged. A door beside the bed led to what she thought must be the en-suite bathroom.

Opposite the entrance door, a pair of french windows gave onto a deep metal-railed balcony. They were flung wide, and Hugo was standing in the opening with his back to the room, a thin blue plume of smoke rising from the cigarette he was holding.

'Just leave it on the table, will you?' he said without turning round.

'Hugo, darling, it's me,' said Claire.

Hugo spun round like a whirling dervish at the sound of her voice.

'Claire! What on earth are you doing here? You're supposed to be in Paris, aren't you? I thought you were the champagne arriving.'

'You seriously thought I'd go to Paris with Richie rather than be here with you?' said Claire. 'The main thing was for you to make a fresh start. That's what you said.'

'I did say that, yes, but . . .'

'But what?' said Claire.

'But not with you,' said Rebecca Maine, stepping out of the en-suite bathroom, towel in hand.

34

For the first time in her life, Claire was genuinely lost for words. Gaping like a fish in a bowl, she turned her head from Hugo to Rebecca and back again. It seemed to her that she had stepped into some kind of parallel universe in which reality had been displaced. Rebecca walked over to Hugo and took his arm.

'It appears you've made a miscalculation, Claire,' she said. 'That's not like you. You're one of the most calculating people I've ever met.'

'I – I don't understand,' said Claire.

'Claire, sit down,' said Hugo, motioning to an armchair. 'You're obviously suffering from some sort of misconception.'

'No,' said Claire as she sat. 'No, I heard you talking to Tim. You said that sleeping with me had made you realise you were obsessed.'

'Obsessed by Rebecca, not with you. Last week I'd attempted to rekindle the relationship with Jane, but I could only think about Rebecca. When I slept with you, I could still only think about Rebecca. That's what I meant by obsessed.'

Claire looked at Rebecca. 'Are you hearing all this? You're the third woman he's slept with in a week.'

'I think you'll find *you're* the third woman, Claire,' said Rebecca. 'Hugo and I have been seeing each other for months. He's a married man. Married men sleep with their wives, and if you're a mistress, as I chose to be, you just have to accept that there are three of you in the relationship. That suited me fine to start with, but as time went by I found myself falling for Hugo in a big way.'

'As did I for Rebecca,' added Hugo, giving her a smile. 'But you know what a rumour mill the hospital is. If our relationship became common knowledge, we'd either have to end it or make it permanent. As I said to you on the phone, Claire, it's not an easy decision to rip up twenty-five years of marriage. Rebecca and I had a long talk and decided that we should have one last evening together and then call it a day.'

'Which left him a free man,' said Rebecca. 'Or a free married man, at least, and me a frustrated woman. Don't you remember how I lost my temper with Iain in the corridor?'

Claire nodded.

'I knew that night was going to be our last.'

'So, you see, we were trying to do the right thing,' said Hugo, 'but I still couldn't get Rebecca out of my head. I thought a diversion might help, and you were so obviously coming on to me, first at Len's party and then on Tim's birthday, that –'

'A diversion! Is that all I was to you?' said Claire.

'Claire, you might be one of the most attractive women in the hospital, but you're also one of the most . . . available. Your band of former lovers is hardly an exclusive club.'

'So you slept with me in an attempt to get over her,' said Claire.

'You might say that,' said Hugo, 'but it was an attempt that failed. I'm the first to admit I've strayed from Jane over the years, but it's always been just a physical thing. With Rebecca, it's much, much more than that. Being with you that night made it clear to me that I couldn't go back to being that person.'

'And so you decided to leave Jane.'

'Yes. You gave me the impression that you knew all this, Claire, when we spoke on the phone. That's why I was so grateful. You're well liked at the hospital, and popular people are opinion makers. If you were supporting our relationship it would give it credence.'

Claire's mind was racing, trying to take this all in. She was nothing if not practical. With Plan A in ruins, was there still a chance to rescue Plan B? She looked at her watch: 5.45. She was already packed; could she get back to the flat before Richie arrived? There might just be time if she –

Her thoughts were interrupted by a knock on the door and a call of 'Room service'.

'Ah, good,' said Hugo. 'I think we could all use a drink.'

The door opened and a white-coated server wheeled in a trolley containing two bottles and crossed quickly to the balcony. Hugo reached for his wallet to tip the man, but as he turned to face the room Claire's world tilted a little further on its axis as she saw that the server was not a server at all. It was Richie, and in his hand was a pistol.

35

Richie placed the pistol on the table and picked up one of the champagne bottles. 'Let's celebrate, shall we?' he said popping the cork and taking a swig. 'Hello, Claire. Fancy seeing you here.' He looked at Rebecca. 'I wasn't expecting you, though. What is it – a threesome? Room for one more?'

'Richie, I can explain,' said Claire. 'This isn't what you think. Hugo and Rebecca are running away together and I'm just –'

'Save your breath, Claire, I know exactly why you're here. Brian told me. And I've been standing outside the door listening for the past ten minutes. It was all I could do to stop myself from laughing out loud. You really are the typical town bike, aren't you? You think you're all that and a bag of chips, but really the only reason any man likes you is that you'll open your legs for him after a glass or two of wine.'

'Look here,' said Hugo, 'there's no need for unpleasantness. I'm sure we can –'

Richie casually lifted the silenced pistol and there was a soft 'pfft' as he fired it at Hugo.

Hugo screamed as blood spurted from his hand.

'Shut up,' said Richie. 'You – bandage him up.' He gestured at Rebecca. 'You're supposed to be a nurse, aren't you?'

Rebecca knelt by Hugo and wrapped her towel around his injured hand.

'Richie, you could have killed him!' shouted Claire. 'What are you even doing with a gun?'

'I belong to a gun club, Claire. It isn't rocket science.'

'No, I mean, why? Why do you need one? No one here is a threat to you.'

Richie laughed. 'Oh, Claire, you really are thick, aren't you? I'm the one holding the weapon; you're the ones being threatened.'

'Because I want someone else more than I want you?' said Claire. 'Really? Christ, talk about bruised male egos.'

'And yet again, Claire Frazer gets it wrong,' said Richie.

'So, enlighten us,' said Rebecca. 'You've got our attention, now get on with the show.'

'You've got some balls, I'll give you that,' said Richie. 'I can see why Mister Fantastic here likes you.'

'Come on, then,' said Rebecca. 'Tell us all what it is she's supposed to have done.'

'She killed two people,' said Richie. 'One of them was my brother.'

'*What?*' said Claire. 'Richie, don't be ridiculous. I haven't killed anyone. You've never said anything to me about having a brother, and I certainly haven't met one.'

'Haven't you? Let me tell you a story, Claire. See if anything jogs your memory. It's Bonfire Night last year. Do you remember it?'

'Of course I remember it. They put on a fireworks party on the bowling green behind the social club. What about it?'

'Anything special happen that you recall?'

Claire shifted uneasily in her seat. 'Nothing unusual, no.'

'Well, nothing unusual for you, perhaps. Just setting your sights on some junior doctor who took your fancy and chatting him up all night so that you could have a quick knee-trembler with him in the bowls club tea room.'

'How did you –'

'Did you know anything about him, Claire?' shouted Richie. 'Did you even ask him his fucking *name*?'

'I don't think so. It was a party, Richie. People were just having a good time,' said Claire.

'Even though he told you his girlfriend would be along later. Even though he begged you to leave him alone, because he was getting married next month. But you kept on and on, didn't you? The irresistible Clare Frazer who loves a challenge. And you got your way, in the end. And what did you do when his girlfriend came looking for him and found you flat on your back with your legs in the air?'

'I don't remember,' said Claire, sobbing. 'Richie, why are you being like this?'

'You *laughed*, Claire. You laughed and told her she was welcome to him.'

'I'm sorry,' said Rebecca, 'but what does all this have to do with anything?'

'Shut up,' said Richie, waving the pistol at her. 'What about her, Claire, the girlfriend? Did you recognise her?'

'It was dark. I couldn't see who it was.'

'I'll tell you, shall I? Her name was Amy Carter, and her fiancé was my brother, Tommy.'

Rebecca gasped. 'The student who killed herself? Len told me about her.'

'The very same. Tommy was broken hearted. He blamed himself. Gave up his studies and went off to do aid work in Africa to atone. While he was there he caught dysentery. He was dead within six weeks. If it hadn't been for you, Claire, he and Amy would have been happily married by now. Instead, they're both six feet under.'

'How do you know that's why Amy killed herself?' asked Rebecca. 'According to Len, there wasn't a note.'

'They didn't find one at the time,' said Richie, 'but when her things were returned to Tommy it was in a pocket of her jeans. He gave it to me. Couldn't bear to keep it, couldn't bear to throw it away. Then he died. I decided someone was going to pay for those two deaths, Claire, and it was going to be you.

'First, I needed to wangle a transfer to my firm's Harvington branch. That took a few months. After that, it was pretty easy to flatter my way into your bed. You don't know how close I came to putting a pillow over your face whenever I stayed over. And I almost literally jumped the gun when I saw the perfect opportunity to stage a tragic accident while we were clay-pigeon shooting. If Charles hadn't come along when he did, you'd have ended up with more holes in you than a colander. But I still had my plan, and I put it into action later that afternoon in the pub. Admittedly, you do have a great body, Claire. I'll confess I did enjoy using it. I can see why Tommy couldn't resist. Just like you, eh, Hugo?'

Hugo said nothing. Claire noticed he was paler than the rising moon outside.

'But to be honest,' Richie continued, 'I was getting tired of it. It was actually quite a relief when that old boy and his dog came along and interrupted our session in the car.'

'So our relationship was never real?' asked Claire. 'All those times you said you loved me . . .'

'False from top to bottom, sweetheart,' said Richie. 'Just like you.'

'And moving in together? Starting a family?'

'The bigger the fantasy castle I could build for you, the more I could enjoy watching it all come crashing down round your ears, just like Amy's real one did,' said Richie.

'But you were so kind, so considerate,' said Claire. 'I really thought we had something, until . . .'

'Until you spotted something better. That sums you up, Claire. You're just an emotional magpie looking for the next shiny thing to pick up and add to your collection.'

His accusation triggered another revelation in her mind. 'And the burglary,' said Claire. 'That was you too, wasn't it?'

'Actually, that was me,' said Rebecca. 'After your floor show at Len's birthday party, I thought I'd check out the competition, see where and how you lived. I had a feeling Hugo and I might eventually get back together, and I wanted to know what I could be up against. Knowledge is power, as they say.'

'So you decided to burgle my flat?' said Claire.

'Not at all,' said Rebecca. 'I'd already learned enough about you from finding out that you lived over a junk shop in a run-down neighbourhood. When I saw your front door gaping wide, though, I couldn't resist taking a look.'

'And stealing my bag. Very classy,' spat Claire.

'A quick look round told me all I needed to know,' Rebecca continued, ignoring her. 'Fake designer labels, kitsch furniture. You're just a wannabe, Claire. Yes, you might have a nice pair of boobs to flash at him, but Hugo is so far out of your league that you were never going to be a serious threat. And I didn't steal your bag. I took it to teach you a lesson. It went straight into the skip at the end of your street. It's probably still there, if you want to dive in and look for it.'

'See, Claire, I'm not the only one to have seen through you,' said Richie.

'My hand,' groaned Hugo. 'It needs attending to.'

'Don't you worry about that. It will soon be the least of your problems,' said Richie.

'What do you mean?' said Hugo, his voice shaking. 'Look, I've got money in the bank. Lots of it. Just name your price and let me walk out of here.'

'Hear that, love?' Richie said to Rebecca. '"Let *me* walk out of here." No mention of you.' He turned to Claire. 'And certainly no mention of *you.* God, you're all swimming in the same self-centred cess pit, aren't you?'

'Richie, we don't have to involve these two,' said Claire.

'They've involved themselves,' he replied. 'I'm sick and tired of people playing emotional football with other people's lives. It's all just a game to you lot, isn't it? Hopping in and out of bed with anyone who takes your fancy. Well, it has consequences, sometimes fatal ones. Two people I loved are dead because you wanted a bit of fun, Claire. And, now it's your turn, all of you.'

'And is killing three people part of your plan?' asked Claire.

'It wasn't, until today. You were supposed to end up committing suicide in a Paris hotel room, hanging yourself from a clothes hook. Sound familiar?'

'Do you think the French police are stupid? They'd arrest you straight away,' said Claire.

'Not when I showed them Amy's suicide note.'

'But my name's not Amy,' said Claire.

'It doesn't have to be. Look, she's even signed it for you.'

He took a piece of paper from his pocket and held it up for her to read.

To whom it may concern.

I'm sorry if this has upset you, but there's only one person to blame for this.

Claire Frazer.

'I was to be the "person to blame" for your suicide, of course, wringing my hands as I confessed my infidelity to the gendarmes. When Brian told me you were running off with Casanova here, though, that all went west. I really didn't know what to do, beyond getting hold of this,' he lifted the pistol, 'and staging some sort of lovers' tiff gone wrong. But this three-way scenario – this is perfect. You arrive here, Claire, the jealous lover, shoot your boyfriend and your rival, then write your goodbye note before turning the gun on yourself. Poor old Hugo will become the "person to blame", while I, of course, will be mortified to find that you have stolen my club-issued pistol to do the deed.'

He waved the gun in the air theatrically. As he did so, Rebecca leapt up from her kneeling position beside Hugo, spun through three hundred and sixty degrees and delivered a kick to his wrist that sent the weapon sailing across the room onto the bed. As Richie made a dive for it she grabbed the full bottle of champagne and broke it over his head. Thirty seconds later, she had trussed her unconscious victim's hands and feet behind his back with the curtain tie-back cords.

'Len wasn't joking when he called you the Karate Kid, Rebecca, was he?' said Claire.

Epilogue

'So,' said Celia, 'come on, tell me everything. We've got six months' catching up to do.'

'Let's go into the garden, shall we?' said Jane. 'I've been baking all morning, and I quite fancy a little afternoon tea outside in the sun. I love May, don't you? Everything seems so fresh and full of promise.'

Six months! Jane thought as she carried out the tea things. Where should she start?

'Tell me about the note,' said Celia, as if reading her mind.

'Oh, Celia, that really was my lowest point. I'd actually decided to end it all after Hugo said he was leaving. But after I'd written that first line –'

'To whom it may concern,' said Celia.

'Yes, after that, I thought about all the people who actually would be concerned. The boys, my parents, you. All these people actually loved me for who I was. If Hugo didn't, well, then he was the one who was misguided – not me. I still had plenty going for me.'

'You go, girl,' said Celia, unleashing one of her deep chuckles. 'And so you wrote the note I found pinned to the door that night. I've still got it here.' She delved into the capacious bag she habitually carried with her and laid a sheet of paper on the table.

To whom it may concern.

I've had enough of being treated like a servant. I'm clearing out the bank account and going travelling. Expect me when you see me.

Jane x

'I laughed so hard when I read that,' said Celia. 'It used to break me up, the way Hugo treated you. And from all the postcards you sent me, it seems that you had a wonderful time.'

'I certainly did, I can tell you, especially the three-month Pacific cruise. Christmas in Samoa is certainly warmer than it is here.'

'These cruises, they can be quite, er, quite romantic, I hear?'

'So I hear,' said Jane. 'But, you know, what happens at sea stays at sea.'

'And all that business at the hotel. I never did get the full story, other than that nurse's boyfriend turned up with a grievance and a gun.'

'Ha, yes. Quite funny, really, in the end. It turned out that this woman Hugo was running off with was a black belt in karate. She knocked the man out while Hugo was cowering in a corner, tied him up like a turkey.'

'Score two for the sisters, then,' said Celia. 'You and her.'

'The police came and carted him off, of course. They found the real waiter tied up in a store cupboard. The boyfriend got seven years for wounding with intent. You can kind of see where he was coming from, though, even if he went about it in completely the wrong way.'

'And the girlfriend? Clara, was it?'

'Claire.'

'That's it, Claire. What happened to her?'

'She had to leave the hospital. Amy Carter had been a popular student, and once everything came out the staff lost all respect for Claire and refused to work under her. Ironically, her deputy didn't want the job and so they promoted Rebecca Maine to lead the department.'

'Karma,' said Celia. 'It always works. So, what's she doing now?'

'She's taken up with her landlord, apparently. Works in his antiques shop.'

'Not much room for infidelity there, then,' said Celia.

'I think she's learned her lesson,' said Jane. 'I feel a bit sorry for her, actually. Her boyfriend was trying to kill her, the man she loved didn't love her and then, to cap it all, she loses her job to her rival.'

'Hello, ladies.'

Both women turned as a figure approached from the house.

'Hello, Hugo,' said Celia.

'Hi, Celia. Lovely to see you. May I?' he asked, cutting himself a slice of fruit cake. 'This really is delicious.'

His movements were awkward, and it took him a while to transfer the slice to a plate.

'Still no use of his right hand, then?' said Celia when he'd gone back inside.

'No, and it's unlikely there ever will be. The bullet did too much damage to the nerves and tendons.'

'Was that why this Rebecca told him she wasn't interested any more?'

'To be honest, I'm not sure. According to one of the girls at the hospital, Rebecca said it was because he'd turned out to be less of a man than she'd thought, but you know what hospital gossip is like.'

'So he came crawling back to you,' said Celia. 'Typical!'

'I haven't exactly taken him back. Not the way you mean, anyway. He was here when I came home from my travels and I let him stay, more for the sake of the boys than anything. There's nothing between us now; he sleeps in the spare room. We're no more than housemates, really. He's just a bit of company.'

'Will you go back to work?' asked Celia.

'I might, just for something to do. I won't need to, of course, not after the insurance payout. That's due any time now.'

'Ah, yes. How much were Hugo's hands insured for again?'

'A million pounds.'

'Wow!' said Celia, and took a large mouthful of cake. 'Hugo's right,' she said once she'd swallowed it, 'this is delicious. He's put on weight, I notice.'

'Yes. He doesn't use the gym any more, or go running. Just sits around the house reading or watching TV.'

Celia nodded.

'Except on Wednesday afternoons. I send him out shopping then. He knows not to come back for a few hours.'

'Why?' said Celia. 'What happens on Wednesdays?'

'That's when my window cleaner comes,' said Jane.

Author's Note

This novel is a work of fiction. Names and characters are the product of the author's imagination and any resemblance to actual incidents or persons, living or dead, is entirely coincidental.

Room Service is my first novel. Thank you so much for reading it; I hope you enjoyed doing so as much as I enjoyed writing it.

I am a mother, grandmother, book lover, cat lover and avid creator. I enjoy stories that are fast-paced and have a bit of frisson to them, and I hope that comes out in my writing.

I like to take inspiration from all areas of my life and have a vivid imagination. Although I have a medical background, I have always maintained my flair and passion for the beautiful things in life and enjoy painting and gardening in my spare time. I also love the great outdoors, and my home in a beautiful Devon seaside town is surrounded by stunning coastal walks and picturesque places that are continuing sources of inspiration.

Reviews are so important to any author. If you enjoyed this book, please consider leaving a review on the site from which you bought it. Thanks for reading!

For upcoming news and giveaways, please subscribe to my email list at **www.bbjamesauthor.com.**

Printed in Great Britain
by Amazon

44230454R00189